Acclaim for **ORHAN PAMUK**

"Think of Kafka with a light touch. . . . A wonderfully fresh voice in the world of fiction."
— *Chicago Sunday Tribune*

"*The White Castle* is an elegant and important meditation on East and West. Comparisons with Kafka and Calvino do not exaggerate; their seriousness, their delicacy and their subtlety are everywhere in evidence."
— *The Independent* (London)

"A new star has risen in the east—Orhan Pamuk. . . . He has earned the right to comparisons with Jorge Luis Borges and Italo Calvino."
— *The New York Times*

"With [his] fusion of literary elegance and incisive political commentary, Pamuk draws comparisons to Salman Rushdie and Don DeLillo."
— *Publishers Weekly*

"Pamuk is a first-rate storyteller. . . . [*The White Castle* is] a highly entertaining, and indeed moving, book with plenty to beguile the reader."
— *The Times Literary Supplement* (London)

Also by **ORHAN PAMUK**

The New Life

The Black Book

ORHAN PAMUK

THE

WHITE CASTLE

Orhan Pamuk is the author of *The New Life* and *The Black Book*. He was born in Istanbul and lives there with his family. His books have been translated into fifteen languages.

INTERNATIONAL

THE
WHITE CASTLE

THE WHITE CASTLE

A Novel by

ORHAN PAMUK

Translated from the Turkish
by Victoria Holbrook

Vintage International
Vintage Books
A Division of Random House, Inc.
New York

FIRST VINTAGE INTERNATIONAL EDITION, APRIL 1998

Library of Congress Cataloging-in-Publication Data

Pamuk, Orhan, 1952–
[Beyaz kale. English]
The white castle : a novel / by Orhan Pamuk ;
translated from the Turkish by Victoria Holbrook.
p. cm.
ISBN 0-375-70161-3
I. Title.
[PL248.P34W4713   1998]
894'.3533—dc21
97-35630
CIP

Printed in the United States of America
10 9 8 7 6

For Nilgun Darvinoglu
a loving sister
(1961–1980)

To imagine that a person who intrigues us has access to a way of life unknown and all the more attractive for its mystery, to believe that we will begin to live only through the love of that person – what else is this but the birth of great passion?

Marcel Proust, from the mistranslation of Y.K. Karaosmanoğlu

Contents

THE
WHITE CASTLE

Preface

I found this manuscript in 1982 in that forgotten 'archive' attached to the governor's office in Gebze that I used to rummage through for a week each summer, at the bottom of a dusty chest stuffed to overflowing with imperial decrees, title deeds, court registers and tax rolls. The dream-like blue of its delicate, marbled binding, its bright calligraphy, shining among the faded government documents, immediately caught my eye. I guessed from the difference in handwriting that someone other than the original calligrapher had later on, as if to arouse my interest further, penned a title on the first page of the book: 'The Quilter's Stepson'. There was no other heading. The margins and blank pages were filled with pictures of people with tiny heads dressed in costumes studded with buttons, all drawn in a childish hand. I read the book at once, with immense pleasure. Delighted, but too lazy to transcribe the manuscript, I stole it from the dump that even the young governor dared not call an 'archive', taking advantage of the trust of a custodian who was so deferential as to leave me unsupervised, and slipped it, in the twinkling of an eye, into my case.

At first I didn't quite know what I would do with the book, other than to read it over and over again. My distrust of history then was still strong, and I wanted to concentrate on the story for its own sake, rather than on the manuscript's scientific, cultural, anthropological, or 'historical' value. I was drawn to the author himself. Since my friends and I had been forced to withdraw from the university, I had taken up my grandfather's profession of encyclopaedist: it was then that it occurred to me to include an entry on the author in the history section – my responsibility – of an encyclopaedia of famous men.

To this task I devoted what spare time remained to me after the encyclopaedia and my drinking. When I consulted the basic sources for the period, I saw right away that some events described in the story bore little resemblance to fact: for example, I confirmed that at one point during the five years Koprulu served as Grand Vizier a great fire had ravaged Istanbul, but there was no evidence at all of an outbreak of disease worth recording, let alone of a widespread plague like the one in the book. Some of the names of viziers of the period had been misspelled, some were confused with one another, some had even been changed. The names of imperial astrologers did not match those in the palace records, but since I thought this discrepancy had a special place in the story I didn't dwell upon it. On the other hand, our 'knowledge' of history generally verified the events in the book. Sometimes I saw this 'realism' even in small details: for example, the historian Naima described in similar fashion the Imperial Astrologer Huseyn Efendi's execution and Mehmet IV's rabbit hunt at Mirahor Palace. It occurred to me that the author, who clearly enjoyed reading and fantasizing, may have been familiar with such sources and a great many other books – such as the memoirs of European travellers or emancipated slaves – and gleaned material for his story from them. He may have merely read the travel journals of Evliya Chelebi, whom he said he knew. Thinking the reverse might just as well be true, as other examples could show, I kept trying to track down the author of my story, but the research I did in Istanbul libraries dashed most of my hopes. I wasn't able to find a single one of all those treatises and books presented to Mehmet IV between 1652 and 1680, neither in the library of Topkapi Palace nor in other public and private libraries where I thought they might have strayed. I came across only one clue: there were other works in these libraries by the 'left-handed calligrapher' mentioned in the story. I chased after them for a while, but only disappointing replies came back from the Italian universities I'd besieged with a torrent of letters; my wanderings among the tombstones of Gebze, Jennethisar, and Uskudar graveyards in search of the name of the author (revealed in the book itself though not on the title-page) were also unsuccessful, and by then I'd had enough: I gave up following possible leads and wrote the encyclopaedia article solely on the basis of the story itself. As I feared, they didn't print this article, not, however, for lack of scientific evidence, but because its subject was not deemed to be famous enough.

My fascination with the story increased even more perhaps for this reason. I even thought of resigning in protest, but I loved my work and my friends. For a time I told my story to everyone I met, as passionately as though I had written it myself rather than discovered it. To make it seem more interesting I talked about its symbolic value, its fundamental relevance to our contemporary realities, how through this tale I had come to understand our own time, etc. When I made these claims, young people usually more absorbed in issues like politics, activism, East-West relations, or democracy were at first intrigued, but like my drinking friends, they too soon forgot my story. A professor friend, returning the manuscript he'd thumbed through at my insistence, said that in the old wooden houses on the back streets of Istanbul there were tens of thousands of manuscripts filled with stories of this kind. If the simple people living in those houses hadn't mistaken them, with their old Ottoman script, for Arabic Korans and kept them in a place of honour high up on top of their cupboards, they were probably ripping them up page by page to light their stoves.

So I decided, encouraged by a certain girl in glasses from whose hand a cigarette was never absent, to publish the story which I returned to read over and over again. My readers will see that I nourished no pretensions to style while revising the book into contemporary Turkish: after reading a couple of sentences from the manuscript I kept on one table, I'd go to another table in the other room where I kept my papers and try to narrate in today's idiom the sense of what remained in my mind. It was not I who chose the title of the book, but the publishing house that agreed to print it. Readers seeing the dedication at the beginning may ask if it has a personal significance. I suppose that to see everything as connected with everything else is the addiction of our time. It is because I too have succumbed to this disease that I publish this tale.

FARUK DARVINOGLU

I

We were sailing from Venice to Naples when the Turkish fleet appeared. We numbered three ships all told, but the file of their galleys emerging from the fog seemed to have no end. We lost our nerve; fear and confusion instantly broke out on our ship, and our oarsmen, most of them Turks and Moors, were screaming with joy. Our vessel turned its bow landward, westward, like the other two, but unlike them we could not gather speed. Our captain, fearing punishment should he be captured, could not bring himself to give the command to whip the captives at the oars. In later years I often thought that this moment of cowardice changed my whole life.

But now it seems to me that my life would have been changed if our captain had *not* suddenly been overcome by fear. Many men believe that no life is determined in advance, that all stories are essentially a chain of coincidences. And yet, even those who believe this come to the conclusion, when they look back, that events they once took for chance were really inevitable. I have reached that moment now, as I sit at an old table writing my book, visualizing the colours of the Turkish ships appearing like phantoms in the fog; this seems the best of times to tell a tale.

Our captain took heart when he saw the other two ships slip away from the Turkish vessels and disappear into the fog, and at last he dared to beat the oarsmen, but we were too late; even whips could not make the slaves obey once they had been aroused by the passion for freedom. Cutting the unnerving wall of fog into waves of colour, more than ten Turkish galleys were upon us at once. Now at last our captain decided to fight, trying to overcome, I believe, not the enemy, but his own fear and shame; he had the slaves flogged mercilessly and ordered the cannons made ready, but the passion for battle, late to flame, was also quick to burn out. We were caught in a violent broadside volley – our ship would surely sink if we did not give up at once – we decided to raise the flag of surrender.

While we waited on a calm sea for the Turkish ships to draw alongside, I went to my cabin, put my things in order as if expecting not arch-enemies who would change my whole life, but a few friends paying a visit, and opening my little trunk rummaged through my books, lost in thought. My eyes filled with tears as I turned the pages of a volume I'd paid dearly for in Florence; I heard shrieks, footsteps rushing back and forth, an uproar going on outside, I knew that at any moment the book would be snatched from my hand, yet I wanted to think not of that but of what was written on its pages. It was as if the thoughts, the sentences, the equations in the book contained the whole of my past life which I dreaded to lose; while I read random phrases under my breath, as though reciting a prayer. I desperately wanted to engrave the entire volume on my memory so that when they did come, I would not think of them and what they would make me suffer, but would remember the colours of my past as if recalling the cherished words of a book I had memorized with pleasure.

In those days I was a different person, even called a different name by mother, fiancée and friends. Once in a while I still see in my dreams that person who used to be me, or who I now believe was me, and wake up drenched in sweat. This person who brings to mind now the faded colours, the dream-like shades of those lands that never were, the animals that never existed, the incredible weapons we later invented year after year, was twenty-three years old then, had studied 'science and art' in Florence and Venice, believed he knew something of astronomy, mathematics, physics, painting. Of course he was conceited: having devoured most of what had been accomplished before his time, he turned up his nose at it all; he had no doubt he'd do better; he had no equal; he knew he was more intelligent and creative than anyone else. In short, he was an average youth. It pains me to think, when I have to invent a past for myself, that this youth who talked with his beloved about his passions, his plans, about the world and science, who found it natural that his fiancée adored him, was actually me. But I comfort myself with the thought that one day a few people will patiently read to the end what I write here and understand that I was not that youth. And perhaps those patient readers will think, as I do now, that the story of that youth who let go of his life while reading his precious books continued later from where it broke off.

When the Turkish sailors threw down their ramps and came on board I put the books in my trunk and peered outside. Pandemonium had broken out on the vessel. They were gathering everyone together on deck and stripping them naked. For a moment it passed through my mind that I could jump overboard in the confusion, but I thought they would shoot me in the water, or capture and kill me immediately, and anyway, I didn't know how close we were to land. At first no one bothered with me. The Muslim slaves, loosed from their chains, were shouting with joy, and a gang of them set about taking vengeance right away on the men who had whipped them. Soon they found me in my cabin, came inside, ransacked my possessions. They rifled through my trunks searching for gold, and after they took away some of my books and all of my clothes, someone grabbed me as I distractedly pored over the couple of books left and took me to one of the captains.

The captain, who as I learned later was a Genoese convert, treated me well; he asked what my profession was. Wanting to avoid being put to the oars, I declared right away that I had knowledge of astronomy and nocturnal navigation, but this made no impression. I then claimed I was a doctor, counting on the anatomy book they'd left me. When I was showed a man who'd lost an arm, I protested that I was not a surgeon. This angered them, and they were about to put me to the oars when the captain, noticing my books, asked if I knew anything of urine and pulses. When I said I did I was saved from the oar and even managed to salvage a few of my books.

But this privilege cost me dear. The other Christians who were put to the oars despised me instantly. They would have killed me in the hold where we were locked up at night if they could have but they were afraid to, because I had so quickly established relations with the Turks. Our cowardly captain had just died at the stake, and as a warning to others they'd cut off the noses and ears of the sailors who'd lashed the slaves, then set them adrift on a raft. After I'd treated a few Turks, using my common sense rather than a knowledge of anatomy, and their wounds had healed by themselves, everyone believed I was a doctor. Even some of those who, moved by envy, had told the Turks I was no doctor at all showed me their wounds at night in the hold.

We sailed into Istanbul with spectacular ceremony. It was said that the child sultan was watching the celebrations. They hoisted their banners on every mast and at the bottom hung our flags, our icons of the Virgin Mary and crucifixes upside down, letting hotheads from the city who jumped aboard shoot at them. Cannon fire burst across the sky. The ceremony, like many I would watch from land in later years with a mixture of sorrow, disgust, and pleasure, lasted such a long time that many spectators fainted in the sun. Towards evening we dropped anchor at Kasimpasha. Before bringing us before the sultan they put us in chains, made our soldiers wear their armour back to front in ridicule, put iron hoops around the necks of our officers, and blasting away on the horns and trumpets they'd taken from our ship, raucously, triumphantly, brought us to the palace. The people of the city were lined up along the avenues, watching us with amusement and curiosity. The

16

sultan, hidden from our view, selected his share of slaves and had them separated from the others. They transported us across the Golden Horn to Galata on caiques and crammed us into Sadik Pasha's prison.

The gaol was a miserable place. Hundreds of captives rotted away in filth inside the tiny, damp cells. I found plenty of people there to practise my new profession on, and I actually cured some of them. I wrote prescriptions for guards with aching backs or legs. So here, too, they treated me differently from the rest, and gave me a better cell that caught the sunlight. Seeing how it was for the others, I tried to be thankful for my own circumstances, but one morning they woke me along with the rest of the prisoners and told me I was going out to work. When I protested that I was a doctor, with knowledge of medicine and science, they just laughed: there were walls to be built around the pasha's garden, men were needed. We were chained together each morning before the sun rose and taken outside the city. While we trudged back to our prison in the evenings, still chained to one another after gathering stones all day, I reflected that Istanbul was indeed a beautiful city, but that here one must be a master, not a slave.

Yet still I was no ordinary slave. People had heard I was a doctor, so now I was not just looking after the slaves rotting away in the prison, but others as well. I had to give a large part of the fees I earned for doctoring to the guards who smuggled me outside. With the money I was able to hide from them, I paid for lessons in Turkish. My teacher was an agreeable, elderly fellow who looked after the pasha's petty affairs. It pleased him to see I was quick to learn Turkish and he'd say I would soon become a Muslim. I had to press him to take his fee after each lesson. I also gave him money to bring me food, for I was determined to look after myself well.

One foggy evening an officer came to my cell, saying that the pasha wished to see me. Surprised and excited, I prepared myself at once. I thought that one of my resourceful

17

relatives at home, perhaps my father, perhaps my future father-in-law, must have sent money for my ransom. As I walked through the fog down the twisting, narrow streets, I felt as if I would suddenly come upon my house, or find myself face to face with my loved ones as though awakening from a dream. Perhaps they had managed to send someone to negotiate my release, perhaps this very night in this same fog I'd be put on a ship and sent back home. When I entered the pasha's mansion I realized I could not be rescued so easily. The people here walked around on tiptoe.

First they led me into a long hall where I waited until I was shown into one of the rooms. An affable little man was stretched out under a blanket on a small divan. There was another, powerfully built man standing at his side. The one lying down was the pasha, who beckoned me to him. We spoke. He asked me a few questions. I said my real fields of study had been astronomy, mathematics, and to a lesser extent engineering, but that I also had knowledge of medicine and had treated a number of patients. He continued to question me and I was about to tell him more when, saying I must be an intelligent man to have learned Turkish so quickly, he added that he had a problem with his health which none of the other doctors had been able to cure, and, hearing of me, he'd wanted to put me to the test.

He began to describe his problem in such a way that I was forced to conclude that it was a rare illness which had stricken only the pasha of all the men on the face of the earth, because his enemies had deceived God with their calumnies. But his complaint was simply shortness of breath. I questioned him at length, listened to his cough, then went down to the kitchen and made mint-flavoured green troches with what I found there. I prepared cough-syrup as well. Because the pasha was afraid of being poisoned, I swallowed one of the troches with a sip of the syrup while he watched. He told me I must leave the mansion secretly, taking great care not to be seen, and return to the prison. The officer later explained that the pasha did not want to arouse the envy of the other doctors. I returned the next day, listened to his cough, and gave him the same medicine. He was as delighted as a child with the colourful troches I left in his palm. As I walked back to my cell, I prayed he would get better. The following day the north wind was blowing. It was a gentle, cool breeze and I thought a man would improve in this weather even against his will, but heard nothing.

A month later when I was called for, again in the middle of the night, the pasha was up on his feet in good spirits. I was relieved to hear him draw breath easily as he scolded a few people. He was glad to see me, said his illness was cured, that I was a good doctor. What favour did I ask of him? I knew he would not immediately free me and send me home. So I complained of my cell, of the prison; explained I was being worn out pointlessly with heavy labour when I could be more useful if I were occupied with astronomy and medicine. I don't know how much of it he listened to. The guards took a lion's share of the purse full of money he gave me.

A week later an officer came to my cell one night, and after making me swear I wouldn't try to escape, took off my chains. I was to be taken out to work again, but the slave-drivers now gave me preferential treatment. Three days later the officer brought me new clothes and I realized I was under the pasha's protection.

I was still being summoned at night to various mansions. I administered drugs to old pirates with rheumatism, and young soldiers whose stomachs ached. I bled those who itched, lost colour, or had headaches. Once, a week after I gave syrups to a servant's stuttering son, he recovered and recited a poem for me.

Winter passed in this way. When spring came I heard that the pasha, who hadn't asked for me in months, was in the Mediterranean with the fleet. During the hot days of summer people who noticed my despair and frustration told me I had no reason to complain, as I was earning good money as a doctor. A former slave who had converted to Islam many years before advised me not to run away. They always kept a slave who was useful to them, as they were keeping me, never granting him permission to return to his country. If I became a Muslim as he had done, I could make a freedman of myself, but nothing more. Since I thought he might have said this just to sound me out, I told him I had no intention of trying to escape. It wasn't the desire I lacked but the courage. Those who fled, all of them, were caught before they got very far. After these unfortunates were beaten I was the one who spread salve on their wounds at night in their cells.

As autumn drew near, the pasha returned with the fleet; he greeted the sultan with cannon fire, tried to cheer the city as he had done the previous year, but it was obvious they'd not passed this season at all well. They brought only a few slaves to the prison. We learned later that the Venetians had burned six ships. Hoping to get news of home, I watched for an opportunity to talk with the slaves, most of whom were Spanish; but they were silent, ignorant, timid things who had no desire to speak unless to beg for help or food. Only one of them interested me: he'd lost an arm, but optimistically said one of his ancestors had lived through the same misadventure and survived to write a romance of chivalry with the arm he had left. He believed he would be spared to do the same. In later years, when I wrote stories to live, I remembered this man who dreamed of living to write stories. Not long after this a contagious disease broke out in the prison, an ill-omened epidemic which killed more than half of the slaves before it passed on, and from which I protected myself by smothering the guards with bribes.

Those left alive were taken out to work on new projects. I didn't go. In the evenings they talked of how they went all the way to the tip of the Golden Horn, where they were set to work at various tasks under the supervision of carpenters, costumers, painters: they were making papier mâché models – ships, castles, towers. Later we learned why: the pasha's son was to marry the daughter of the grand vizier and he was arranging a spectacular wedding.

One morning I was called to the pasha's mansion. I went, thinking his shortness of breath had returned. The pasha was engaged, they took me to a room to wait, I sat down. After a few moments another door opened and someone five or six years older than myself came in. I looked up at his face in shock – immediately I was terrified.

2

The resemblance between myself and the man who entered the room was incredible! It was *me* there... for that first instant this was what I thought. It was as if someone wanted to play a trick on me and had brought me in again by a door directly opposite the one I had first come through, saying, look, you really should have been like this, you should have come in the door like this, should have gestured with your hands like this, the other man sitting in the room should have looked at you like this. As our eyes met, we greeted one another. But he did not seem surprised. Then I decided he didn't resemble me all that much, he had a beard; and I seemed to have forgotten what my own face looked like. As he sat down facing me, I realized that it had been a year since I last looked in a mirror.

After a few moments the door through which I had entered opened and he was called inside. While I waited, I thought this must be all a fiction of my troubled mind rather than a cleverly planned joke. For in those days I was always fantasizing that I would return home, welcomed by all, that they would immediately set me free, that actually I was still asleep in my cabin on the ship, it had all been a dream – consoling visions of that sort. I was about to conclude that this, too, was one of those day-dreams, but one come to life, or that it was a sign that everything would suddenly change and return to its former state, when the door opened and I was summoned inside.

The pasha was standing up, a little behind my look-alike. He let me kiss the hem of his skirt, and I intended when he enquired after my welfare to mention my sufferings in my cell, that I wanted to return to my country, but he wasn't listening. It seemed that the pasha remembered I'd told him I had knowledge of science, astronomy, engineering – well then, did I know anything of those fireworks hurled at the sky, of gunpowder? Immediately I replied that I did, but the instant my eyes met those of the other man I suspected they were leading me into a trap.

The pasha was saying that the wedding he planned would be unparalleled, and he would have a fireworks display, but it must be quite unlike any other. My look-alike, whom the pasha called only 'Hoja', meaning 'master', had in the past, at the sultan's birth, worked on a display with fire-eaters arranged by a Maltese who had since died, so he knew a little about these things, but the pasha thought I would be able to assist him – we would complement one another. The pasha would reward us if we put on a good display. When, thinking the time had come, I dared to say that what I wanted was to return home, the pasha asked me if I'd been to a whorehouse since I arrived, and hearing my answer, said if I had no desire for a woman what good would freedom be to me? He was using the coarse language of the guards and I must have looked bewildered, for he roared with laughter. Then he turned to that spectre he called 'Hoja': the responsibility was his. We left.

In the morning as I walked to my look-alike's house I imagined there was nothing I would be able to teach him. But apparently his knowledge was no greater than mine. Moreover, we were in accord: the whole problem was to come up with the right camphoric mixture. Our task would thus be to carefully prepare experimental mixtures with scale and measures, fire them off at night in the shadows of the high city walls at Surdibi, and derive conclusions from what we observed. Children watched our men in awe while they ignited the rockets we'd prepared, and we stood under the dark trees waiting anxiously for the result, just as we would do years later by daylight while testing that incredible weapon. After these experiments I would try, sometimes by moonlight, sometimes in blind darkness, to record our observations in a small notebook. Before separating for the night, we'd return to Hoja's house overlooking the Golden Horn and discuss the results at length.

His house was small, oppressive, and unattractive. The entrance was on a crooked street muddied by a dirty stream flowing from some source I was never able to discover. Inside there was almost no furniture, but every time I entered the house I felt pressed in and overcome by a queer feeling of distress. Perhaps it came from this man who, because he didn't like being named after his grandfather, wanted me to call him 'Hoja': he was watching me, he seemed to want to learn something from me, but wasn't yet sure what it was. Since I could not get used to sitting on the low divans that lined the walls, I stood up while we discussed our experiments, sometimes pacing nervously up and down the room. I believe Hoja enjoyed this. He could sit and watch me to his heart's content, if only by the dim light of a lamp.

As I felt his eyes following me it made me all the more uneasy that he didn't notice the resemblance between us. Once or twice I thought he saw it but was pretending not to. It was as if he were toying with me; he was performing a small experiment on me, obtaining information I couldn't comprehend. For in those first days he continually scrutinized me as if he were learning something and the more he learned the more curious he became. But he seemed hesitant to take any further steps to penetrate the meaning of this strange knowledge. It was this inconclusiveness that oppressed me, that made the house so suffocating! True, I gained some confidence from his hesitation, but it did not reassure me. Once, while we were discussing our experiments, and another time when he asked me why I still had not become a Muslim, I felt he was covertly trying to draw me into an argument so I did not respond. He sensed my restraint; I realized he thought less of me for it, and this made me angry.

In those days it was perhaps only in this way we understood each other: each of us looked down on the other. I held myself in check, thinking that if we succeeded in putting on the fireworks display without mishap, they would grant me permission to return home.

One night, elated by the success of a rocket that had climbed to an extraordinary height, Hoja said that someday he would be able to make one that would shoot as high as the moon; the only problem was to find the requisite proportions of gunpowder and cast a chamber that could tolerate the mixture. I remarked that the moon was very far away but he interrupted me, saying he knew that as well as I, but wasn't it also the planet nearest the Earth? When I admitted he was right, he didn't relax as I expected, he became even more agitated, but said nothing more.

Two days later, at midnight, he took up the question again: how could I be so sure that the moon was the closest planet? Perhaps we were letting ourselves be taken in by an optical illusion. It was then I spoke to him for the first time about my studies in astronomy and explained briefly the basic principles of Ptolemaic cosmography. I saw that he listened with interest, but was reluctant to say anything that would reveal his curiosity. A little later, when I stopped talking, he said he too had knowledge of Ptolemy but this did not change his suspicion that there might be a planet nearer than the moon. Towards morning he was talking about that planet as if he had already obtained proofs of its existence.

The next day he thrust a badly translated manuscript into my hand. In spite of my poor Turkish I was able to decipher it: I believe it was a second-hand summary of *Almageist* drawn up not from the original but from another summary; only the Arabic names of the planets interested me, and I was in no mood to get excited about them at that time. When Hoja saw I was unimpressed and soon put the book aside, he was angry. He'd paid seven gold pieces for this volume, it was only right that I should set aside my conceit, turn the pages and take a look at it. Like an obedient student, I opened the book again and while patiently turning its pages came across a primitive diagram. It showed the planets in crudely drawn spheres arranged in relation to the Earth. Although the positions of the spheres were correct the illustrator had no idea of the distances between them. Then my eye was caught by a tiny planet between the moon and the Earth; examining it a little more carefully, I could tell from the relative freshness of the ink that it had been added to the manuscript later. I went over the entire manuscript and gave it back to Hoja. He told me he was going to find that planet: he did not seem at all to be joking. I said nothing, and there was a silence that unnerved him as much as it did me. Since we were never able to make another rocket shoot high enough to steer the conversation to astronomy again, the subject was not re-opened. Our little success remained a coincidence whose mystery we could not solve.

But we had very good results with the violence and brightness of light and flame, and we knew the secret of our success: in one of the herbalist shops Hoja searched out one by one he'd found a powder even the shop-owner did not know the name of; we decided that this yellowish dust, which produced a superb brightness, was a mixture of sulphur and copper sulphate. Later we mixed the powder with every substance we could think of to give brilliance to the effect, but we were unable to obtain anything more than a coffee-coloured brown and a pale green barely distinguishable from one another. According to Hoja, even this was infinitely better than anything Istanbul had ever seen.

And so was our display on the second night of the celebration, everyone said so, even our rivals who intrigued behind our backs. I was very nervous when we were told that the sultan had come to watch from the far shore of the Golden Horn, terrified something might go wrong and that it would be years before I could return to my country. When they ordered us to begin, I said a prayer. First, to welcome the guests and announce the beginning of the display, we fired off colourless rockets shooting straight up into the sky; immediately after that we set off the hoop display Hoja and I called 'The Mill'. In an instant the sky turned red, yellow and green, booming with terrifying explosions. It was even more beautiful than we'd hoped; as the rockets soared the hoop gathered speed, whirled and whirled and suddenly, lighting up the surrounding area bright as day, hung suspended, motionless. For a moment I thought I was in Venice again, an eight-year-old watching a fireworks display for the first time and just as unhappy because it was not I who was wearing my new red suit, but my big brother who'd torn his own clothes in a quarrel the previous day. The exploding fireworks were as red as the bright buttoned suit I couldn't wear that night and swore I never would again, the same red as the matching buttons on the suit which was too tight for my brother.

Then we set off the display we called 'The Fountain'; flames poured from the mouth of a scaffold the height of five men; those on the far shore should have had a good view of the streaming flames; they must have been as excited as we were when the rockets began to shoot out of the mouth of 'The Fountain', and we did not intend to let their excitement die down: the caiques on the surface of the Golden Horn stirred. First the papier mâché towers and fortresses, shooting rockets from their turrets as they sailed by, caught fire and went up in flames – these were supposed to symbolize victories of former years. When they released the ships representing those from the year I'd been taken captive, other ships attacked our vessel with a rain of rocket fire; thus I relived the day I had become a slave. As the ships burned and sank, shouts of 'God, oh God!' arose from both shores. Then, one by one, we released our dragons; flames spurted from their huge nostrils, their gaping mouths and pointed ears. We had them fight one another; as planned, none could defeat the other at first. We reddened the sky even more with rockets fired from shore, and after the sky

27

had darkened a bit, our men on the caiques turned the winches and the dragons began to ascend very slowly into the sky; now everyone was screaming in fear and awe; as the dragons attacked one another again with a great uproar, all the rockets on the caiques were fired at once; the wicks we had placed in the bodies of the creatures must have caught fire at just the right moment, for the whole scene, exactly as we desired, was transformed into a burning inferno. I knew we had succeeded when I heard a child screaming and weeping nearby; his father had forgotten the boy and was staring open-mouthed at the terrible sky. At last I will be allowed to return home, I thought. Just then, the creature I called 'The Devil' glided into the inferno on a little black caique invisible to the eye; we had tied so many rockets to it that we were afraid all the caiques might blow up, along with our men, but everything went as planned; as the battling dragons disappeared into the sky, spitting flames, 'The Devil' and its rockets, all catching fire at once, swooped into the heavens; balls of fire scattering from every part of its body exploded, booming in the air. I exulted at the thought that in one moment we had managed to terrify all Istanbul. I was afraid as well, just because I seemed to have at last found the courage to do the things I wanted in life. At that moment it seemed of no importance what city I was in; I wanted that devil to hang suspended there, showering fire over the crowd all night long. After swaying a little from side to side, it fluttered down upon the Golden Horn without harming anyone, accompanied by ecstatic screams from both shores. It was still spewing fire from its top as it sank into the water.

The next morning the pasha sent Hoja a purse of gold, just as in fairy tales. He had said he was very pleased with the display but found the victory of 'The Devil' strange. We continued the fireworks for ten more nights. By day we repaired the burnt models, planned new spectacles and had captives brought from the prison to fill rockets. One slave was blinded when ten bags of gunpowder exploded in his face.

After the wedding celebrations were over, I saw Hoja no more. I felt easier away from the probing eyes of this curious man who watched me constantly, but it wasn't as if my mind didn't wander back to the exhilarating days we'd spent together. When I returned home, I would tell everyone about the man who looked so much like me and yet had never referred to this haunting resemblance. I sat in my cell, looking after patients to pass the time; when I heard the pasha had called for me I felt a thrill, almost happiness, and ran to go. First he praised me perfunctorily, everyone had been satisfied with the fireworks, the guests were pleased, I was quite talented, etc. Suddenly he said that if I became a Muslim he would make me a freedman at once. I was shocked, stupefied, I said I wanted to return to my country, in my folly I even went so far as to stutter a few sentences about my mother, my fiancée. The pasha repeated what he'd said as if he had not heard me at all. I kept silent for a while. For some reason I was thinking of lazy, good-for-nothing boys I'd known in childhood; the sort of wicked children who raise their hands against their fathers. When I said I would not abandon my faith, the pasha was furious. I returned to my cell.

Three days later, the pasha called for me again. This time he was in a good mood. I had reached no decision, being unable to decide whether changing my religion would help me to escape or not. The pasha asked for my thoughts and said he himself would arrange for me to marry a beautiful girl here. In a sudden moment of courage, I said I would not change my religion, and the pasha, surprised, called me a fool. After all, there was no one around me whom I would be ashamed to tell I had become a Muslim. Then he talked for a while about the precepts of Islam. When he had finished, he sent me back to my cell.

On my third visit I was not brought into the pasha's presence. A steward asked for my decision. Perhaps I would have changed my mind, but not because a steward asked me to! I said I was still not ready to abandon my faith. The steward took me by the arm and brought me downstairs, surrendering me to someone else. This was a tall man, thin like the men I often saw in my dreams. He also took me by the arm, and as he was leading me to a corner of the garden, kindly as though helping a bedridden invalid, someone else came up to us, this one too real to appear in a dream, a huge man. The two men, one of whom carried a smallish axe, stopped at the foot of a wall and tied my hands: they said the pasha had commanded that I should be beheaded at once if I would not become a Muslim. I froze.

Not so quickly, I thought. They were looking at me with pity. I said nothing. At least don't let them ask me again, I was saying to myself, when a moment later they did ask. Suddenly my religion became something that seemed easy to die for; I felt I was important, and on the other hand I pitied myself the way these two men did who made it harder for me to abandon my religion the more they interrogated me. When I tried to think of something else the scene through the window overlooking the garden behind our house came to life before my eyes: peaches and cherries lay on a tray inlaid with mother-of-pearl upon a table, behind the table was a divan upholstered with straw matting strewn with feather cushions the same colour as the green window-frame; further back, I saw a sparrow perched on the edge of a well among the olive and cherry trees. A swing tied with long ropes to a high branch of a walnut-tree swayed slightly in a barely perceptible breeze. When they asked me once again, I said I would not change my religion. They pointed to a stump, made me kneel and lay my head upon it. I closed my eyes, but then opened them again. One of them lifted the axe. The other said perhaps I had regretted my decision: they stood me up. I should think it over a while longer.

Leaving me to reconsider, they began to dig into the earth next to the stump. It occurred to me they might bury me here right now, and along with the fear of death, I now felt the fear of being buried alive. I was telling myself I'd make up my mind by the time they finished digging the grave when they came towards me, having dug only a shallow hole. At that moment I thought how very foolish it would be to die here. I felt I could become a Muslim, but I had no time to form a resolve. If I'd been able to return to the prison, to my beloved cell I'd finally grown used to, I could have sat up all night thinking and made the decision to convert, but not like this, not right away.

They seized me suddenly, pushing me to my knees. Just before I laid my head on the stump I was bewildered to see someone moving through the trees, as if flying; it was me, but with a long beard, walking silently on the air. I wanted to call out to the apparition of myself in the trees, but I could not speak with my head pressed against the stump. It will be no different from sleep, I thought, and let myself go, waiting; I felt a chill at my back and the nape of my neck, I didn't want to think, but the cold at my neck made me go on. They stood me up, grumbling that the pasha would be furious. As they untied my hands they admonished me: I was the enemy of God and Muhammad. They took me up to the mansion.

After letting me kiss the hem of his skirt, the pasha treated me gently; he said he loved me for not abandoning my faith to save my life, but a moment later he started to rant and rave, saying I was being stubborn for nothing, Islam was a superior religion, and so on. The more he chastised me the angrier he became; he had decided to punish me. He began to explain he'd made a promise to someone, I understood that this promise spared me sufferings I would otherwise have endured, and finally realized that the man to whom the promise had been made, an odd man judging from what he said, was Hoja. Then the pasha said abruptly that he had given me to Hoja as a present. I looked at him blankly; the pasha explained that I was now Hoja's slave, he'd given Hoja a document, the power to make me a freedman or not was now his, he would do whatever he liked with me from now on. The pasha left the room.

I was told that Hoja **was** at the mansion too, waiting for me downstairs. I realized then that it was he I had seen through the trees in the garden. We walked to his house. He said he'd known all along I wouldn't abandon my faith. He'd even made ready a room in his house for me. He asked if I were hungry. The fear of death was still upon me, I was in no state to eat anything. Still I was able to get down a few mouthfuls of the bread and yogurt he put before me. Hoja watched happily while I chewed my food. He looked at me with the pleasure of a peasant feeding a fine horse he'd just bought from the bazaar, thinking of all the work it would do for him in future. Until the days when he forgot me, submerged in the details of his theory of cosmography and designs for the clock he planned to present to the pasha, I had many occasions to remember that look.

Later he said I would teach him everything; that's why he'd asked the pasha to give me to him, and only after I had done this would he make me a freedman. It would take me months to find out what this 'everything' was. 'Everything' meant all that I'd learned in primary and secondary school; all the astronomy, medicine, engineering, everything that was taught in my country. It was what was written in the books in my cell he had a servant go and fetch the following day, all I'd heard and seen, all I had to say about rivers, bridges, lakes, caves and clouds and seas, the causes of earthquakes and thunder... Around midnight he added that it was the stars and planets which most interested him. Moonlight was shining in through the open window, he said we must at least find definite proof regarding the existence or non-existence of that planet between the moon and the Earth. With the ravaged eyes of a man who'd spent a day standing side by side with death, I couldn't help but notice the unnerving likeness between us again as Hoja gradually ceased to use the word 'teach': we were going to search together, discover together, progress together.

So, like two dutiful students who work faithfully at their lessons even when the grown-ups are not at home listening through a cracked door, like two obedient brothers, we sat down to work. In the beginning I felt more like the solicitous elder who agrees to review his old lessons so as to help his lazy little brother catch up; and Hoja behaved like a clever boy who tries to prove that the things his big brother knows are really not all that much. According to him, the gap between his knowledge and mine was no greater than the number of volumes he'd had brought from my cell and lined up on a shelf and the books whose contents I remembered. With his phenomenal diligence and quickness of mind, in six months he'd acquired a basic grasp of Italian which he'd improve upon later, read all of my books, and by the time he'd made me repeat to him everything I remembered, there was no longer any way in which I was superior to him. However, he acted as if he had access to a knowledge that transcended what was in books – he himself agreed most of them were worthless – a knowledge more natural and more profound than things that could be learned. At the end of six months we were no longer companions who studied together, progressed together. It was he who came up with ideas, and I would only remind him of certain details to help him along or review what he already knew.

He more often found these 'ideas', most of which I have forgotten, at night, long after we'd finished the improvised meal we ate in the evening and all the lamps in the neighbourhood had gone out, leaving everything around us wrapped in silence. In the mornings he'd go to teach at the primary school in the mosque a couple of neighbourhoods away, and two days a week he'd go to a faraway district I'd never set foot in and stop by the clock-room of a mosque, where the times of prayer are calculated. The rest of our time we spent either preparing for the night's 'ideas' or chasing after them in pursuit. At that time I still had hope, I believed I would soon return home, and since I felt that to debate the particulars of his 'ideas', to which I listened with little interest, would, if anything, delay my return, I never openly disagreed with Hoja.

So we passed the first year, burying ourselves in astronomy, struggling to find proofs of the existence or non-existence of the imaginary planet. But while he worked to design telescopes for the lenses he imported from Flanders at great expense, invented instruments and drew up tables, Hoja forgot the question of the planet; he had become involved in a more profound problem. He would dispute Ptolemy's system, he said, but we didn't engage in disputation; he talked while I listened: he said it was folly to believe that the planets hung from transparent spheres; there was something else that held them there, an invisible force, a force of attraction perhaps; then he proposed that the Earth might, like the sun, be revolving around something else, perhaps all the stars turned around some other heavenly centre of whose existence we had no knowledge. Later, claiming his ideas would be far more comprehensive than Ptolemy's, he included a number of new planets in his observations for a much wider cosmography, producing theories for a new system; perhaps the moon revolved around the Earth, and the Earth around the sun; perhaps the centre was Venus; but he quickly grew tired of these theories. He had just come to the point of saying that the problem now was not to suggest these new ideas but to make the stars and their movements known to men here – and he would begin this task with Sadik Pasha – when he learned that the pasha had been banished to Erzurum. It seems he'd been involved in an abortive conspiracy.

During the years we waited for the pasha to return from exile, we researched a treatise Hoja would write about the causes of the Bosphorus currents. We spent months observing the tides, roaming the cliffs overlooking the straits in a wind that chilled us to the bone, and descending into the valleys with the pots we carried to measure the temperature and flow of the rivers that emptied into the straits.

While in Gebze, a town not far from Istanbul where we'd gone at the pasha's request for three months to look after some business of his, the discrepancies between times of prayer at the mosques gave Hoja a new idea: he would make a clock that would show the times of prayer with flawless accuracy. It was then that I taught him what a table was. When I brought home the piece of furniture I'd had made by a carpenter according to my specifications, Hoja was not pleased. He likened it to a four-legged funeral bier, said it was inauspicious, but later he grew accustomed both to the chairs and the table; he declared he thought and wrote better this way. We had to go back to Istanbul to have gears for the prayer clocks cast in an elliptical shape corresponding to the arc of the setting sun. On the return journey our table, its legs pointing to the stars, followed us on the back of a mule.

In those first months, while we sat facing one another at the table, Hoja tried to work out how to calculate the times of prayer and fasting in northern countries where there was a great variation in the duration of day and night and a man went for years without seeing the face of the sun. Another problem was whether or not there was a place on earth where people could face Mecca whichever way they turned. The more he realized that I was indifferent to these problems, the more contemptuous he became, but I thought at the time that he discerned my 'superiority and difference', and perhaps he was irritated because he believed that I, too, was aware of it: he talked about intelligence as much as he did about science; when the pasha returned he would gain favour by his plans, his theories of cosmography which he would develop further and then demonstrate by means of a model, and by the new clock; he would infect all of us with the curiosity and enthusiasm that burned in him, he would sow the seeds of a new revival: we were, both of us, waiting.

3

In those days he was thinking about how to develop a larger geared mechanism for a clock which would require setting and adjusting only once a month rather than once a week. After developing such a geared apparatus, he had it in mind to devise a clock that would need adjustment only once a year; finally he announced that the key to the problem was to provide enough power to drive the cogwheels of this great timepiece, which had to increase in number and weight according to the amount of time between settings. That was the day he learned from his friends at the mosque clock-room that the pasha had returned from Erzurum to take up a higher office.

Hoja went to congratulate him the following morning. The pasha singled him out among the throng of visitors, showed interest in his discoveries, and even asked after me. That night we dismantled and rebuilt the clock over and over again, adding a few things here and there to the model of the universe, painting in the planets with our brushes. Hoja read to me parts of a speech he painstakingly composed and then memorized, which was intended to move his listeners by sheer force of elegant language and poetic ornament. Towards morning, in order to calm his nerves, he recited to me once more this piece of rhetoric about the logic of the turning of the planets but this time he recited it backwards, like an incantation. Loading our instruments on a wagon he'd borrowed, he left for the pasha's mansion. I was stunned to see how the clock and the model, which had filled the house for months, now appeared so tiny on the back of the one-horse cart. He returned very late that evening.

After he'd unloaded the instruments in the garden of the mansion and the pasha had examined these odd objects with the severity of a disagreeable old man in no mood for jokes, Hoja immediately recited to him the speech he'd memorized. The pasha, alluding to me, had said, as the sultan would say many years later: 'Was it he who taught you these things?' This was his only response at first. Hoja's reply surprised the pasha even more: 'Who?' he'd asked, but then understood that the pasha was referring to me. Hoja told him that I was a well-read fool. As he narrated this he gave no thought to me, his mind was still on what had happened in the pasha's mansion. He'd insisted that everything was his own discovery, but the pasha had not believed him, he seemed to be looking for someone else to blame and his heart would not allow that his beloved Hoja was the guilty party.

This was how they'd come to talk about me instead of the stars. I could see that it had not pleased Hoja to discuss this subject. There had been a silence while the pasha's attention was drawn to the other guests around him. At dinner, when Hoja made another attempt to bring up astronomy and his discoveries, the pasha said that he'd been trying to recall my face, but instead Hoja's had come to his mind. There had been others at table, a prattling began on the subject of how human beings were created in pairs, hyperbolic examples on this theme were recalled, twins whose mothers could not tell them apart, look-alikes who were frightened at the sight of one another but were unable, as if bewitched, ever again to part, bandits who took the names of the innocent and lived their lives. When dinner was over and the guests were leaving, the pasha had asked Hoja to stay.

When Hoja had begun to talk again, the pasha seemed hardly entertained at first, even displeased at having his good mood upset again with a lot of mixed-up information that did not appear to be comprehensible, but later, after listening for a third time to the speech Hoja recited by heart, and watching the Earth and stars of our orrery turn, rolling around before his eyes, he seemed to have taken in a thing or two, at least he began to listen attentively to what Hoja was saying, showing just the slightest bit of curiosity. At that point Hoja had repeated vehemently that the stars were not as everyone believed, that this was how they turned. 'Very well,' the pasha said at last, 'I understand, this too is possible, why not, after all.' In response Hoja had said nothing.

I imagined there must have been a long silence. Hoja spoke, looking out the window into the darkness over the Golden Horn. 'Why did he stop there, why didn't he go further?' If this were a question, I didn't know the answer any better than he did: I suspected that Hoja had an opinion about what more the pasha might have said, but he said nothing. It was as if he were upset that other people did not share his dreams. The pasha had later become interested in the clock, he'd asked him to open it up and explain the purpose of the cogs, the mechanism, and its counterweight. Then fearfully, as if approaching a dark and disgusting snake-hole, he'd put a finger into the ticking instrument and withdrawn it. Hoja had been talking about clock-towers, praising the power of prayer performed by every-one at exactly the same perfect moment, when suddenly the pasha erupted. 'Be rid of him!' he'd said. 'If you like, poison him, if you like, free him. You'll be more at ease.' I must have glanced at Hoja with fear and hope for a moment. He said he would not free me until 'they' realized.

I didn't ask what it was that 'they' must realize. And perhaps I had a premonition which made me afraid I might find that Hoja didn't know what it was either. Later they'd talked of other things, the pasha was frowning and looking contemptuously at the instruments before him. Hoja remained at the mansion into the late hours of the night, waiting in the hope that the pasha's interest would revive, though he knew he was no longer welcome. At last he had loaded his instruments onto the cart. I pictured someone in a house along the dark, silent road back, lying in bed unable to sleep: wondering at the sound of the huge clock ticking amidst the clatter of the wheels.

Hoja stayed up until the break of day. I wanted to replace the dying candle, but he stopped me. Because I knew he wanted me to say something, I said, 'The pasha will understand.' I said this while it was still dark, perhaps he knew as well as I did that I didn't believe it, but a moment later he spoke up, saying the whole problem was to unravel the mystery of that moment when the pasha had stopped talking.

In order to solve this mystery, he went to see the pasha at the first opportunity. He had greeted Hoja cheerfully this time. He said he'd understood what had happened, or what was intended, and after soothing Hoja's feelings advised him to work on a weapon. 'A weapon to make the world a prison for our enemies!' That is what he had said, but he hadn't said what kind of thing this weapon should be. If Hoja turned his passion for science in this direction, then the pasha would support him. Of course he'd said nothing about the endowment we hoped for. He simply gave Hoja a purse full of silver coins. We opened it at home and counted the money: there were seventeen coins – a strange number! It was after giving him this purse that he'd said he would persuade the young sultan to grant Hoja an audience. He explained that the child was interested in 'such things'. Neither I nor Hoja, who was more easily enthused, took his promise very seriously, but a week later there was news. The pasha was going to present us, yes, me as well, to the sultan, after the evening breaking of the fast.

In preparation Hoja revised and memorized again the speech he'd recited for the pasha, changed this time so that a nine-year-old child could understand it. But for some reason his mind was on the pasha, not the sultan, he was still wondering why the pasha had fallen silent. He would discover the secret of this one day. What kind of thing could this weapon be that the pasha wanted made? There was little left for me to say, Hoja was working on his own now. While he stayed locked up in his room till midnight, I sat vacantly at my window, not even thinking of when I would return home but daydreaming like a foolish child: it was not Hoja but I who was working at the table, free to go wherever, whenever I wished!

Then one evening we loaded our instruments on to a wagon and went off to the palace. I'd come to love walking the streets of Istanbul, I felt like an invisible man moving like a ghost among the giant plane-trees, the chestnut and erguvan trees in the gardens. We set up the instruments with the help of attendants, on the site they pointed out to us in the second courtyard.

The sovereign was a sweet, red-cheeked child of a height proportionate to his few years. He handled the instruments as if they were his toys. Am I thinking now of that time when I wanted to be his peer and friend, or of another time much later, fifteen years later, when we met again? I cannot tell; but I felt immediately that I must do him no wrong. Hoja suffered a bout of nerves while the sultan's entourage waited, crowding round in curiosity. At last he was able to begin; he'd added new things to his tale; he talked about the stars as if they were intelligent, living beings, likening them to attractive, mysterious creatures who knew arithmetic and geometry, and who revolved in accord with their knowledge. He grew more passionate as he saw that the child was affected and raised his head from time to time to look at the sky in wonder. See, the planets hung on the turning transparent spheres were represented in the model there, there was Venus and it revolved this way and the huge ball hanging there was the moon and it, you understand, followed a different course. While Hoja made the stars turn, the bell attached to the model tinkled with a sweet sound and the little sultan, scared, took a step back, then, gathering his courage, made an effort to understand

and approached the ringing machine as if it were an enchanted treasure-chest.

Now, as I recollect my memories and try to invent a past for myself, I find this a portrait of happiness fit for the fables I heard as a child, exactly as the painters of the pictures in those fairy-tale books would have it. The gingerbread-red roofs of Istanbul need only be encased in those glass spheres that swirl with snow when you shake them. The child had begun to ask Hoja questions, and he to find answers for them.

How did the stars stay in the air? They hung from the transparent spheres! What were the spheres made of? Of an invisible material, so they were invisible too! Didn't they bump into one another? No, each had its own zone, layered as in the model! There were so many stars, why weren't there as many spheres? Because they were very far away! How far? Very, very! Did the other stars have bells that rang when they turned? No, we attached the bells to mark each complete revolution of the stars! Did thunder have any relation to this? None! What did it relate to? Rain! Was it going to rain tomorrow? Observation of the sky showed it would not! What did the sky reveal about the sultan's ailing lion? It was going to get better, but one must be patient, and so on.

While he gave his opinion about the ailing lion, Hoja continued to look at the sky, as he did when he talked about the stars. After returning home he mentioned this detail, saying that it didn't matter. The important thing was not that the child distinguish between science and sophistry, but that he should 'realize' a few things. He was using the same word again, as if I understood what it was he should realize, while I was thinking it would make no difference whether I became a Muslim or not. There were exactly five pieces of gold in the purse they gave us as we left the palace. Hoja said the sultan had grasped that there was a logic behind what happened in the stars. O my sultan! later, much later did I know him! It amazed me that the same moon appeared through the window of our house, I wanted to be a child! Hoja, unable to stop himself, returned to the same subject: the question of the lion was not important, the child loved animals, that was all.

The next day he shut himself up in his room and began to work: a few days later he loaded the clock and the stars on to the wagon again and, under the gaze of those curious eyes behind the latticed windows, went this time to the primary school. When he returned in the evening he was depressed, but not so much as to keep silent: 'I thought the children would understand as the sultan did, but I was wrong,' he said. They had only been frightened. When Hoja had asked questions after his lecture, one of the children replied that Hell was on the other side of the sky and began to cry.

He spent the next week bolstering his confidence in the sovereign's intelligence; he went over with me one by one every moment that we had spent in the second courtyard, getting my support for his interpretations: the child was clever, yes; he already knew how to think, yes; he was already possessed of enough character to withstand the pressure put upon him by those around him at court, yes! Thus long before the sultan began to dream for us, as he would in later years, we began to dream for him. Hoja was working on the clock, too, at this time; I believed he was also thinking a bit about the weapon, because he said so to the pasha when he was called to see him. But I could tell that he'd given up on the pasha. 'He's become like the others,' he said. 'He no longer wants to know that he doesn't know.' A week later the sovereign summoned Hoja again, and he went.

The sultan had received Hoja in good spirits. 'My lion is better,' he'd said, 'it is as you predicted.' Later they'd gone out into the courtyard with his retinue. The sovereign, showing him the fish in the pool, had asked what he thought of them. 'They were red,' Hoja said when he told me about it. 'I couldn't think of anything else to say.' Then he'd noticed a pattern to the movements of the fish; it was as if they were actually discussing the pattern among themselves, trying to perfect it. Hoja had said he found the fish to be intelligent. When a dwarf, standing next to one of the harem eunuchs who continually reminded the sovereign of his mother's admonitions, laughed at this, the sultan rebuked him. As punishment he didn't allow the red-headed dwarf to sit next to him when he ascended to his carriage.

They'd gone by carriage to the hippodrome, to the lion-house. The lions, leopards, and panthers the sultan showed Hoja one by one were chained to the columns of an ancient church. They stopped in front of the lion Hoja had predicted would get well, the child spoke to it, introducing the lion to Hoja. Then they'd gone to another lion lying in a corner, this animal, not filthy-smelling like the others, was pregnant. The sovereign, his eyes shining, asked, 'How many cubs will this lion give birth to, how many will be male, how many female?'

Taken by surprise, Hoja did something he later described to me as a 'blunder'. He told the sultan he had knowledge of astronomy but was not an astrologer. 'But you know more than Imperial Astrologer Huseyn Efendi!' the child had said. Hoja didn't answer, fearing someone nearby might hear and pass it on to Huseyn Efendi. The impatient sovereign had insisted: or did Hoja know nothing, did he observe the stars in vain after all?

In response Hoja was forced to explain at once things that he'd intended to say only much later: he replied he had learned many things from the stars and arrived at very useful conclusions based on what he'd learned. Interpreting favourably the silence of the sovereign, who was listening with widening eyes, he said it was necessary to build an observatory to watch the stars; like that observatory his grandfather Ahmet the First's grandfather, Murat the Third, had built for the late Takiyuddin Efendi ninety years ago, and which later fell into ruin from neglect. Or rather, something more advanced than that: a House of Science where scholars could observe not only the stars, but the whole world, its rivers and oceans, clouds and mountains, flowers and trees and, of course, its animals, and then come together to discuss their observations at leisure and make progress in the advance of the intellect.

The sultan had listened to Hoja talk of this project which I, too, was hearing about for the first time, as if listening to an agreeable fable. As they returned to the palace in their carriages he'd asked once again, 'How will the lion give birth, what do you say?' Hoja had thought it over and this time answered, 'An equal number of male and female cubs will be born.' At home he told me there was no danger in having said this. 'I will have that fool of a child in the palm of my hand,' he said. 'I am more adept than the Imperial Astrologer Huseyn Efendi!' It shocked me to hear him use this word in speaking of the sovereign; for some reason I even took offence. In those days I was keeping myself occupied with housework out of boredom.

Later he began to use that word as if it were a magical key that would unlock every door: because they were 'fools' they didn't look at the stars moving over their heads and reflect on them, because they were 'fools' they asked first what was the good of the thing they were about to learn, because they were 'fools' they were interested not in details but in summaries, because they were 'fools' they were all alike, and so on. Although I too had liked to criticize people this way, not many years before, when I still lived in my own country, I'd say nothing to Hoja. At the time, in any case, he was preoccupied with his fools, not with me. Apparently my folly was of another kind. In my indiscretion those days I had told him of a dream I'd had: he had gone to my country in my place, was marrying my fiancée, at the wedding no one realized that he was not me, and during the festivities which I watched from a corner dressed as a Turk, I met up with my mother and fiancée who both turned their backs on me without recognizing who I was, despite the tears which finally wakened me from the dream.

Around that time he went twice to the pasha's mansion. I believe the pasha was not pleased to find Hoja developing a relationship with the sovereign away from his watchful eye; he'd interrogated him; he'd asked after me, he'd been investigating me, but only much later, after the pasha had been banished from Istanbul, did Hoja tell me this; he feared I might have passed my days in terror of being poisoned if I had known. Still, I could tell that the pasha was more intrigued by me than he was by Hoja; it flattered my pride that the resemblance between Hoja and myself disturbed the pasha more than it did me. In those days it was as if this resemblance were a secret Hoja would never wish to know and whose existence lent me a strange courage: sometimes I thought that by grace of this resemblance alone I would be safe as long as Hoja lived. Perhaps that is why I contradicted Hoja when he'd say the pasha, too, was one of those fools; he became irritated at that. He spurred me to a brazenness I was not accustomed to, I wanted to feel both his need for me and his shame before me: I relentlessly questioned him about the pasha, about what he said regarding the two of us, strangling Hoja in a rage the cause of which I believe was not clear even to him. Then he'd stubbornly repeat that they would get rid of the pasha too, soon the janissaries would be up to something, he sensed the presence of conspiracies within the palace. For this reason, if he were going to work on a weapon as the pasha suggested, he should build it not for some vizier who would come and go, but for the sultan.

For a while I thought he was occupied exclusively with this obscure notion of a weapon; planning but not getting anywhere, I said to myself. For had he made progress, I was sure he'd have shared it with me, even if trying to belittle me while doing so, he would have told me about his designs in order to learn my opinion. One evening we were returning home after going to that house in Aksaray where we listened to music and lay with prostitutes, as we did every two or three weeks. Hoja said he was planning to work till morning, then asked me about women – we had never talked about women – and said suddenly, 'I'm thinking...' but the moment we entered the house he shut himself up in his room without revealing what was on his mind. I was left alone with the books I now had no desire even to browse through, and thought of him: of whatever plan or idea he had that I was convinced he could not develop, of him shut up in the room sitting at the table to which he was still not completely accustomed, staring at the empty pages before him, sitting fruitlessly at the table for hours in shame and rage...

He emerged from his room well after midnight and like an embarrassed student needing help with some minor question that defeated him, sheepishly called me inside to the table. 'Help me,' he said abruptly. 'Let's think about them together, I can't make any progress on my own.' I was silent for a moment, thinking this had something to do with women. When he saw me look blank he said seriously, 'I'm thinking about the fools. Why are they so stupid?' Then, as if he knew what my answer would be, he added, 'Very well, they aren't stupid, but there is something missing inside their heads.' I didn't ask who 'they' were. 'Don't they have any corner inside their heads for storing knowledge?' he said, and looked around as if searching for the right word. 'They should have a compartment inside their heads, some compartment like the drawers of this cabinet, a spot where they can put various things, but it's as if there were no such place. Do you understand?' I wanted to believe I had understood a thing or two, but couldn't quite succeed in this. For a long time we sat facing one another in silence. 'Who can know why a man is the way he is anyway?' he said at last. 'Ah, if only you'd been a real physician and taught me,' he went on, 'about our bodies, the insides of our bodies and our heads.' He seemed a bit embarrassed. With an air of good humour which I thought he feigned because he didn't want to frighten me, he announced that he was not going to give up, he would go on to the end, both because he was curious about what would happen and because there was nothing else to do. I understood nothing, but it pleased me to think he'd learned all of this from me.

Later he often repeated what he'd said, as if we both knew what it meant. But despite the conviction he affected, he had the air of a daydreaming student posing questions; every time he said he would go on till the end I'd feel I was witnessing the mournful, angry complaints of a hapless lover asking why all this had befallen him. In those days he said this very often; he said it when he learned the janissaries were plotting a rebellion, said it after he told me the students in the primary school were more interested in angels than in stars, and after another manuscript he paid a considerable sum for was thrown aside in a rage before he'd read it even halfway through, after parting from his friends in the mosque clock-room with whom he now got together merely out of habit, after freezing in the badly heated baths, after stretching out on his bed with his beloved books strewn over the flowered quilt, after listening to the idiotic chatter of the men making their ablutions in the mosque courtyard, after learning that the fleet had been beaten by the Venetians, after listening patiently to the neighbours who came to call saying he was getting old and should marry, he repeated it again: he would go on till the end.

Now I begin to wonder: who, once having read what I've written to the end, patiently following everything I have been able to convey of what happened, or of what I have imagined, what reader could say that Hoja did not keep this promise he made?

4

One day near the end of summer we heard that the body of the Imperial Astrologer Huseyn Efendi had been found floating by the shores of Istinye. The pasha had at last obtained the order for his death, and the astrologer, unable to keep quiet, betrayed his hiding place by sending letters near and far saying Sadik Pasha would soon die, it was written in the stars. When he attempted to escape to Anatolia the executioners overtook his boat and strangled him. As soon as Hoja learned that the dead man's property had been seized, he rushed to get his hands on the papers and books; for this he spent all his savings on bribes. One evening he brought home a huge trunk filled with thousands of pages and after devouring these in just one week, said angrily that he could do much better.

I assisted him as he laboured to make good his word. For two treatises he had decided to write for the sovereign, entitled *The Bizarre Behaviour of The Beasts* and *The Curious Wonders of God's Creatures*, I described to him the fine horses and the donkeys, rabbits, and lizards I had seen in the spacious gardens and meadows on our estate at Empoli. When Hoja remarked that my powers of imagination were all too limited, I remembered the mustachioed French turtles in our lily-pond, the blue parrots that talked with Sicilian accents, and the squirrels who would sit facing one another preening their coats before mating. We devoted much time and care to a chapter on the behaviour of ants, a subject which fascinated the sultan but which he could not learn enough about because the first courtyard of the palace was continually being swept.

As Hoja wrote of the orderly, logical life of ants, he nurtured a dream that we might educate the young sultan. Finding our native black ants inadequate for this purpose, he described the behaviour of American red ants. This gave him the idea to write a book that would be entertaining as well as instructive about the lazy aborigines who lived in that snake-ridden country called America and never changed their ways: I suppose he did not dare finish this book in which he said, as he described it to me in detail, that he would also write how a child-king fond of animals and hunting was ultimately impaled at the stake by Spanish infidels because he paid no attention to science. The drawings by a miniaturist we employed to give a vivid representation of winged buffalo, six-legged oxen, and two-headed snakes, satisfied neither of us. 'Reality may have been flat like that in the old days,' said Hoja. 'But now everything is three-dimensional, reality has shadows, don't you see; even the most ordinary ant patiently carries his shadow around on his back like a twin.'

Hoja received no communication from the sultan and so decided to ask the pasha to present the treatises on his behalf, but he later regretted this. The pasha gave him a lecture, saying that astrology was sophistry, that the Imperial Astrologer Huseyn Efendi had got in over his head by mixing himself up in politics and that he suspected Hoja now had his eye on the position left empty, that he himself believed in this thing called science but it was a matter of weapons, not stars, that the office of imperial astrologer was an inauspicious one as was clear from the fact that all who occupied it were murdered sooner or later, or worse, vanished into thin air, and he therefore did not want his beloved Hoja, whose science he relied upon, to take up this position, that in any case the new imperial astrologer would be Sitki Efendi, who was stupid and simple enough to do this job, that he'd heard Hoja had obtained the former astrologer's books and he wanted him not to bother himself further with this affair. Hoja replied that he concerned himself only with science and gave the pasha the treatises he wanted conveyed to the sultan. That evening at home he said that indeed he did care only for science, but would do whatever was necessary in order to practise it; and for a start he cursed the pasha.

During the next month we tried to guess the child's reaction to the colourful animals of our fancy, while Hoja wondered why he had still not been called to the palace. At last we were summoned to the hunt; we went to Mirahor Palace on the shores of Kagithane River, he to stand at the sovereign's side, I to watch from afar; a great crowd had gathered. The imperial gamekeeper had prepared well: rabbits and foxes were let loose and greyhounds set on their heels, and we watched while all eyes followed one of the rabbits as it drew away from its fellows and threw itself into the water; when, swimming frantically, it reached the far shore, the gamekeepers wanted to let more dogs loose there as well, but even we at our distance could hear the sovereign withhold his permission with the order: 'Let the rabbit go free.' However, the rabbit jumped into the water again and a wild dog on the far shore chased and caught it, but the gamekeepers rushed forward to rescue it from the dog's jaws and brought it into the sultan's presence. The child examined the animal at once and was gratified to find no serious wound; he ordered that the rabbit be taken to a mountain-top and set free. Then I saw a group including Hoja and the red-headed dwarf gather around the sovereign.

That evening Hoja explained to me what happened: the sultan had asked how the event should be interpreted. After everyone else had spoken and Hoja's turn came, he said it meant that enemies would emerge from quarters the sultan least expected, but he would survive the threat unscathed. When Hoja's rivals, among them the new Imperial Astrologer Sitki Efendi, criticized this interpretation for raising the spectre of death – even going so far as to compare the sovereign with a rabbit – the sultan silenced them all saying he would take Hoja's words as the earring for his ear. Later, while they watched a black eagle attacked by falcons fight for its life, and saw the pitiful death of a fox mauled by ravenous hounds, the sultan said that his lion had given birth to two cubs, one male and one female, an equal number as Hoja had predicted, that he loved Hoja's bestiaries, and asked about the bulls with blue wings and the pink cats who live in the meadows near the Nile. Hoja was intoxicated with a strange mixture of triumph and fear.

Only much later did we hear of the mischief at the palace: the sultan's grandmother, Kosem Sultana, had conspired with the janissary aghas in a plot to murder him and his mother, and have Prince Suleyman put on the throne in his place, but the plot failed. They strangled her till the blood flowed from her mouth and nose. Hoja learned all this from the gossip of the fools at the clock-room in the mosque, and he continued his teaching at the school, but otherwise did not venture from the house.

In the autumn for a while he considered working on his cosmographical theories again but lost faith: he needed an observatory; moreover the fools here cared as little for the stars as the stars do for fools. Winter came, dark clouds hung heavy in the sky, and one day we learned the pasha had been dismissed from office. He too was to have been strangled, but the sultan's mother would not consent and he was instead banished to Erzinjan, his property confiscated. We heard nothing more about him until his death. Hoja said he now feared no one, he owed a debt to no man – I don't know how much consideration he gave to whether he'd learned anything from me when he said this. He claimed he no longer feared either the child or his mother. He felt ready to cast dice with death and glory, but we sat at home among our books quiet as lambs, talking about American red ants and dreaming up a new treatise on the subject.

We passed that winter at home like so many before and so many to come; nothing at all happened. On the cold nights when the north wind blew down the chimney and under the doors we would sit downstairs talking till dawn. He no longer belittled me, or couldn't be bothered to act as if he did. I attributed his new comradeship to the fact that no one sought him out, neither from the palace nor from the palace circle. At times I thought he perceived the uncanny resemblance between us as much as I did, and I was worried that when he looked at me now he saw himself: what was he thinking? We had finished another long treatise on animals, but since the pasha's banishment this lay on the table, while Hoja said he wasn't ready to put up with the caprices of those who had access to the palace. Now and then, idle as the days passed without incident, I would leaf through the pages of the treatise looking at the violet grass-hoppers and flying fish I'd drawn, wondering what the sultan would think when he read these lines.

Only when spring came was Hoja finally summoned. The child had been very pleased to see him; according to Hoja it was obvious from his every gesture, his every word, that the sultan had long been thinking of him, but was prevented by the idiots at court from seeking him out. The sovereign spoke of his grandmother's treachery, saying Hoja had foreseen the threat but had also foreseen that the sultan would survive unharmed. That night in the palace the child had not been in the least afraid when he heard the shouts of those who meant to murder him, because he'd remembered that vicious dog had not harmed the rabbit in its jaws. After these words of praise he ordered that Hoja be granted the income from a suitable piece of land. Hoja had to leave before the subject of astronomy could arise; he was told to expect the grant at summer's end.

While he waited, Hoja made plans to build a small obser-vatory in the garden, anticipating the income from the land. He calculated the dimensions of the foundations to be dug and the price of the instruments he would require, but he quickly lost interest this time. It was then he found a poorly transcribed manuscript in the old book bazaar, recording the results of Takiyuddin's observations. He spent two months testing the accuracy of the observations, but in the end gave up in disgust, unable to determine which discrepancy was due to the shortcomings of his inferior instruments, which to Takiyuddin's own errors, and which to the carelessness of the scribe. What irritated him even more were the verses a former owner of the book had scribbled between the trigonometric columns calculated in degrees of sixty. The former owner, using numerical values of the alphabet and other methods, offered his humble observations on the future of the world: in the end a male child would be born to him after four females, a plague would strike dividing the innocent from the guilty, and his neighbour Bahaeddin Efendi would die. Although Hoja was at first amused by these predictions, he later grew depressed. He now talked about the insides of our heads with a strange and ominous conviction: it was as if he were talking about trunks with lids one could open and look inside, or about the cupboards in our room.

The grant promised by the sultan did not come at the end of summer, nor yet as winter approached. The next spring Hoja was told a new deed register was being prepared; he must wait. During this time he was invited to the palace, though not very often, to offer his interpretations of such phenomena as a mirror that cracked, a bolt of green lightning which struck the open sea around Yassi Island, a blood-red crystal decanter filled with cherry juice which splintered to smithereens where it stood, and to answer the sovereign's questions about the animals in the last treatise we had written. When he came home he would say that the sovereign was entering puberty; this was the most impressionable stage of a man's life, he would have that child in the palm of his hand.

With this goal in mind he started afresh on a completely new book. He had learned from me of the fall of the Aztecs and the memoirs of Cortez, and had in mind even before that the story of a pathetic child-king who was impaled at the stake because he paid no heed to science. He often talked of the immoral wretches who, with their cannon and machines of war, their deceiving tales and their weapons, ambushed honourable men while they slept and forced them to submit to their rule; but for a long time he hid from me whatever it was he shut himself up to write. I could tell that at first he expected me to show interest, but in those days my intense longing for home, which would suddenly plunge me into the most extraordinary gloom, had increased my hatred for him; I suppressed my curiosity, pretended not to care about the dusty books with torn bindings he read because he got them cheap, and to disdain the conclusions his creative intellect derived from what I had taught him. Day by day he gradually lost confidence, first in himself, then in what he was trying to write, while I watched with vindictive pleasure.

He'd go upstairs to the little room he'd made his private study, sit at our table which I'd had built, and think, but I sensed that he wasn't writing, I knew he could not; I knew he didn't have the courage to write without first hearing my opinion of his ideas. It was not exactly want of my humble thoughts, which he pretended to scorn, that made him lose faith in himself: what he really wanted was to learn what 'they' thought, those like me, the 'others' who had taught me all that science, placed those compartments, those drawers full of learning inside my head. What would they think were they in his situation? It was this he was dying to ask, but couldn't bring himself to do so. How long I waited for him to swallow his pride and find the courage to ask me this question! But he didn't ask. He soon abandoned this book. I could not tell whether he'd finished writing or not, and resumed his old refrain about the 'fools'. He would renounce his belief that the fundamental science worthy of practice was the one which would analyse the causes of their folly; renounce the desire to know why the insides of their heads were like they were, and stop thinking about it! I believed these broodings were born of his despair because the signs of favour he expected from the palace did not appear. Time passed in vain, the sovereign's puberty wasn't much help after all.

But in the summer before Koprulu Mehmet Pasha became grand vizir, Hoja received the grant at last; and it was one he might have chosen himself: he'd been granted the combined income from two mills near Gebze and two villages an hour's ride from that town. We went to Gebze at harvest time, taking our old house which by chance stood empty, but Hoja had forgotten the months we'd passed there, the days when he looked with distaste at the table I brought home from the carpenter. His memories seemed to have grown old and ugly along with the house: in any case he was consumed with an impatience that made it impossible for him to care for anything in the past. On a few occasions he went to inspect the villages; he calculated the income earned in previous years, and influenced by Tarhunju Ahmet Pasha, whom he'd heard about from his friends' gossip at the mosque clock-room, he announced that he'd found a new system for keeping an accounts' ledger in a much simpler and more readily understandable fashion.

But the originality and usefulness of this innovation, in which even he did not believe, was not enough for him: the wasted nights he spent sitting in the garden behind the old house looking at the sky rekindled his passion for astronomy. I encouraged him for a while, believing he'd take his theories a step further; but his intention was not to make observations or use his mind: he invited the most intelligent youths he knew from the village and from Gebze to the house, saying he'd teach them the highest science, set up for them in the back garden the orrery he'd sent me to Istanbul to retrieve, repaired the bells, oiled it, and one evening, with an enthusiasm and energy he got from I don't know where, passionately repeated, without omission or error, that theory of the heavens he'd expounded years before first to the pasha and then to the sultan. But when the next morning we found a sheep's heart on our doorstep, still warm and bleeding, with a spell written upon it, this was enough to make him finally give up all hope both in the youths who'd left the house at midnight without asking one question, and in astronomy.

But he did not dwell on this setback either: surely they were not the ones to understand the turning of the earth and stars; for now it was not necessary that they should understand; the one who must understand was about to grow out of puberty, and perhaps he had sought us in our absence, we were missing our opportunity for the sake of the few pennies we'd receive here after the harvest. We settled our affairs, hired the most intelligent-looking of those bright youths as overseer, and returned to Istanbul.

The next three years were our worst. Every day, every month, was like the one before, every season a sickening, nerve-racking repetition of some other season we'd lived through: it was as if we painfully, desperately, watched the same things happening again, waiting in vain for some disaster we could not name. He was still called to the palace now and then, where they expected him to provide his inoffensive interpretations, and still gathered with his friends in science at the mosque clock-room on Thursday afternoons, still saw his students in the mornings and beat them, even if not as regularly as before, still resisted those who came to the house now and then with offers of marriage, even if not quite as decisively as he used to, still was obliged to listen to that music he said he didn't like anymore in order to lie with the women, still sometimes seemed about to choke on the hatred he felt for his fools, still would shut himself in his room, lie down on the bed he spread out, thumb irritably through the pages of the manuscripts and books stacked all around him and wait, staring at the ceiling for hours on end.

What made him even more miserable were the victories of Koprulu Mehmet Pasha he heard about from his friends at the mosque clock-room. When he told me the fleet had routed the Venetians, or that the islands of Tenedos and Limnos had been recaptured, or that the rebel Abaza Hasan

56

Pasha had been crushed, he'd add that these were the last of merely fleeting successes, the pathetic wrigglings of a cripple soon to be buried in the slime of idiocy and incompetence: he seemed to be waiting for some disaster to change the monotony of these days that exhausted us all the more as they repeated one another. Worse, since he no longer had the patience and confidence to concentrate on the thing he obstinately called 'science', he had nothing to distract him: he could not keep his enthusiasm for a new idea for more than one week, he soon remembered his fools and forgot all else. Wasn't the thought he'd devoted to them till now enough? Was it worth wearing himself out over them? Worth getting so angry? And perhaps, since he had only just learned to set himself apart from them, he could muster neither the strength nor desire to investigate this science in detail. He had begun, however, to believe he was different from the others.

His first impression was born of sheer frustration. By now, because he could not concentrate on any subject for long, he passed his time like a spoiled and stupid child who cannot amuse itself, wandering from room to room in the house, up and down the staircase from one floor to the other, gazing absently from this window or that. When he would pass by me during this endless, maddening to and fro that made the floors of the wooden house groan and creak in protest, I knew he hoped I would distract him with some joke, some novel idea or encouraging word. But despite my sense of defeat, the anger and hatred I felt for him had lost none of their force and I would not respond. Even when, to get some sort of answer out of me, he swallowed his pride and met my intractability humbly, with a few kind words, I wouldn't say what he longed to hear; when he announced he had information from the palace that could be favourably interpreted, or was struck by a new idea that could be worth its weight in gold if he persisted and followed it up, I either pretended not to hear him or doused his enthusiasm at once by emphasizing the most insipid thing in what he said. I enjoyed watching him struggle in the vacuum of his own mind.

But later he found in this very emptiness the new idea he needed; perhaps because he was left to his own devices, perhaps because his mind, unable to be still, could not escape its own rampant impatience. It was then that I gave him an answer – I wanted to encourage him – my interest too was aroused; perhaps while this was going on I even thought he cared for me. One evening when Hoja's steps creaked through the house to my room and he said, as if asking the most ordinary sort of question, 'Why am I what I am?' I wanted to encourage him and tried to answer.

I replied that I didn't know why he was what he was, adding that this question was often asked by 'them', and asked more and more every day. When I said this I had nothing to support it, no particular theory in mind, nothing at all but a desire to answer his question as he wished, perhaps because I sensed instinctively that he would enjoy the game. He was surprised. He eyed me with curiosity, he wanted me to continue; when I remained silent he couldn't restrain himself, he wanted me to repeat what I'd said: So they ask this question? When he saw me smile in approval he immediately became angry: he wasn't asking this because he thought 'they' asked it, he'd asked it on his own without knowing they did, he couldn't care less what they did. Then, in a strange tone he said, 'It's as if a voice were singing in my ear.' This mysterious voice reminded him of his beloved father, he'd heard a voice like that too before he died, but his song had been different. 'Mine keeps singing the same refrain,' he said, and seeming a bit embarrassed, added suddenly, 'I am what I am, I am what I am, ah!'

I almost laughed out loud, but controlled the impulse. If this were a harmless joke then he should laugh too; he wasn't laughing; but he realized that he was on the verge of appearing ridiculous. I had to show that I was aware both of the absurdity and the meaning of the refrain; for this time I wanted him to go on. I said the refrain should be taken seriously; of course, the singer he heard was none other than himself. He must have found some hint of ridicule in what I said, for he became angry: he too knew that; what mystified him was why the voice kept on repeating this phrase!

He was so agitated that of course I didn't tell him, but frankly, this is what I was thinking: I knew, not only from my own experience but from that of my brothers and sisters, that the boredom selfish children experience could lead either to productive results or to nonsense. I said it was not why he heard this refrain, but what it meant that he should consider. Perhaps it also occurred to me then that he might go mad for lack of anything to fix upon; and that I could escape the oppression of my own despair and cowardice by watching him. Then again, perhaps this time I would genuinely be able to respect him; if he could do this, something real might now happen in both our lives. 'So what should I do?' he asked helplessly at last. I told him he should think about why he was what he was, and that I did not say this because I presumed to give him advice; I wouldn't be able to help him, this was something he had to do for himself. 'So what should I do, look in the mirror?' he said sarcastically. But he didn't seem any less upset. I said nothing, to give him time to think. 'Should I look in the mirror?' he repeated. Suddenly I was angry, I felt Hoja would never be able to achieve anything on his own. I wanted him to realize this, I wanted to tell him to his face that without me he could not think at all, but I didn't dare; with an air of indifference I told him to go ahead and look in the mirror. No, it wasn't courage I lacked, I just didn't feel like it. He flew into a rage and slammed the door, shouting as he left: You are a fool.

Three days later when I brought up the subject again and saw he still wanted to talk about 'them', it pleased me to continue the game; whatever might come of it, it gave me hope just to see him occupied with something. I said 'they' did look in the mirror, and in fact much more often than people here did. Not only the palaces of kings, princes, and noblemen, but the homes of ordinary people as well were full of mirrors carefully framed and hung upon the walls; it wasn't only because of this but because 'they' constantly thought about themselves that 'they' had progressed in this respect. 'In what?' he asked, with an eagerness and innocence that surprised me. I thought he was taking what I said seriously, but then he grinned: 'So you mean that they gaze in mirrors from morning till night!' For the first time he was mocking my country and what I had left behind. Angrily, I searched for something to say to hurt him, and suddenly, without thinking, without believing it, I declared that only he could discover who he was, but he wasn't man enough to try. It gave me pleasure to see his face contort with pain.

But this pleasure would cost me dear. Not because he threatened to poison me; a few days later, he demanded that I demonstrate the courage I'd said he lacked. At first I tried to make a joke of it; of course, a person could no more discover who he was by thinking about it than by looking in a mirror; I'd said that in anger to annoy him; but he seemed not to believe me: he threatened to feed me less, even to lock me in the room if I did not prove my courage. I must work out who I was and write it down; he would see how it was done, see how much courage I had.

5

At first I wrote a few pages about my happy childhood with my brothers and sisters, my mother and grandmother on our estate at Empoli. I didn't know just why I chose to write about these memories in particular as a way of discovering why I was who I was; perhaps I was prompted by the longing I must have felt for the happiness of that life I'd lost; and Hoja had so pressed me after what I'd said in anger that I was obliged, just as I am now, to dream up something my reader would find believable and to try to make the details enjoyable. But at first Hoja didn't like what I wrote; anyone could write things like this, he said; he doubted this was what people thought about when they contemplated themselves in the mirror, for this could not be the courage I had said he lacked. His response was the same when he read about how I suddenly came face to face with a bear on a hunting expedition in the Alps with my father and brothers, and we'd stood still staring at one another for a long time, or how I'd felt at the deathbed of our beloved coachman who was trampled by his own horses before our eyes: anyone could write these things.

To this I replied that people there did no more than this, what I'd said before was exaggerated, I'd been angry, and Hoja should not expect more of me. But he wasn't listening; I dreaded being locked in the room and so continued writing down the images that came to mind. In this way I spent two months reviving and reviewing, sometimes painfully, sometimes happily, a host of memories of this kind, all minor, but pleasant to remember. I imagined and relived

61

the good and the bad experiences I'd had before I became a slave, and in the end I realized I had enjoyed the exercise. Now Hoja didn't have to force me to write; every time he said he was not satisfied, I'd go on to another memory, to another tale I'd decided on beforehand to write down.

Much later, when I noticed that Hoja enjoyed reading what I'd written as well, I began to watch for an opportunity to draw him into this activity. To prepare the ground I spoke of certain experiences I'd had in childhood: I told him about the terrors of an endless, sleepless night following the death of my closest friend with whom I'd got into the habit of thinking the same thing at the same time, how I feared that I might be presumed dead and be buried alive with him. I didn't expect he would be so taken by this! Soon after I dared to tell him a dream I'd had: my body separated itself from me, joined with a look-alike of mine whose face was veiled by shadows, and the two of them conspired together against me. At the time Hoja had been saying he was hearing that ridiculous refrain again and more intensely. When I saw that, as I'd hoped, he was affected by the dream, I insisted that this kind of writing was something he too should try. It would distract him from this endless anticipation, and he would discover what it was that truly set him apart from his fools. He was called to the palace from time to time, but there were no encouraging developments there. At first he resisted, but when I pressed him, he was curious, embarrassed and fed up enough to say he would try it. He was afraid of being found ridiculous and even jokingly asked me: just as we wrote together, would we also look at ourselves in the mirror together?

When he said he wanted us to write together, I had no idea he would actually want to sit together at the table. I had thought that when he started to write I would get back to the idle freedom of an indolent slave. I was wrong. He said we must sit at the two ends of the table and write facing one another: our minds, confronted by these dangerous subjects, would drift, trying to escape, and only in this way would we start on the path, only in this way could we strengthen each other with the spirit of discipline. But these were excuses; I knew he was afraid to be left alone, to feel his own solitude while he was thinking. I saw this also by the way he began to mumble, just loud enough for me to hear, when he came face to face with the blank page; he was waiting for me to approve beforehand what he was going to write. After scrawling a few sentences, he showed them to me with the innocent humility and eagerness of a child: were these things worth writing about, he wondered? Naturally I gave my approval.

Thus in the space of two months I learned more about his life than I'd been able to learn in eleven years. His family had lived in Edirne, a city we later visited with the sovereign. His father died very young. He couldn't be sure he remembered his face. His mother had been a hard-working woman. She remarried after his father died. She had two children by her first husband, one girl and one boy. By her second husband she'd had four sons. This man had been a quilter. The child most inclined to study had of course been himself. I learned that he also had been the most intelligent, cleverest, most diligent, and the strongest of his brothers; he had also been the most honest. He remembered all of them with hatred, except for his sister, but he wasn't quite sure it was worth writing all of this down. I encouraged him, perhaps because I already sensed then that I would later adopt his manner and his life-story as my own. There was something in his language and his turn of mind that I loved and wanted to master. A person should love the life he has chosen enough to call it his own in the end; and I do. He thought all his brothers were fools, of course; they only sought him out to get money from him; he, however, had given himself over to study. Accepted at the Selimiye seminary, he'd been falsely accused just as he was about to graduate. He never referred to this incident again, nor did he ever speak of women. At the very beginning he wrote that he'd once been on the point of marrying, then angrily ripped up everything he'd written. There was a filthy rain falling that night. It was the first of many terrifying nights I would later endure. He insulted me, said what he'd written was a lie, and began all over again; and since he required that I sit facing him and write also, I went for two days without sleep. He no longer took any notice of what I wrote; I sat at the other end of the table, copying what I had written, without bothering to use my imagination, and watched him out of the corner of my eye.

A few days later, on that expensive, immaculate paper imported from the East, he began with the title 'Why I Am What I Am', but under this heading, every morning, he wrote nothing but reasons why 'they' were so inferior and stupid. Still, I did learn that after his mother's death he'd been cheated, had come to Istanbul with what money he salvaged from his inheritance, stayed at a dervish house for a while but left when he decided that all the people there were base and false. I wanted to get him to tell me more about his experiences at the dervish house; I thought that breaking away from them had been a real success for him: he'd been able to set himself apart from them. When I said this he became angry, said I wanted to hear sordid things so I could use them against him some day; I had already learned too much anyway, and on top of this it made him suspicious that I wanted to learn those details – here he used one of those sexual expressions considered coarse. Then he talked for a long time about his sister Semra, of how virtuous she was and how wicked her husband had been; he spoke of his regret at not seeing her for so many years, but when I showed interest in this he became suspicious again, and passed on to another topic: after he'd spent what money he had on books, he did nothing but study for a long time, later found work as a scribe here and there – but people were so shameless – and then he remembered Sadik Pasha, whose death had just been reported from Erzinjan. Hoja had met him for the first time then, and immediately had caught his eye with his love of science. The pasha had found

Hoja his teaching job at the primary school, but he was just another fool. At the end of this bout of writing, which lasted a month, one night, ashamed, he tore to shreds everything he'd written. It's because of that, as I try to reconstruct his scribblings and my own experiences, relying only on my imagination, I'm not frightened any more of being overwhelmed by details that fascinate me so much. In a last burst of enthusiasm he wrote a few pages organized under the heading 'Fools I Have Known Well', but then flew into a rage: all of this writing had got him nowhere; he'd learned nothing new, and he still didn't know why he was what he was. I had deceived him, I'd made him think pointlessly about things he didn't want to remember. He was going to punish me.

I don't know why this idea of punishment, which recalled our first days together, so preoccupied him. Sometimes I thought my cowardly obedience had made him bold. Yet the moment he spoke of punishment, I made the decision to stand up to him. When Hoja had become completely fed up with writing about the past, he paced up and down the house for a while. Then he came to me again and said it was thought itself that we must write down: just as man could view his appearance in a mirror. he could examine his essence within his own thoughts.

The bright symmetry of the analogy excited me as well. We sat down immediately at the table. This time I too, though half ironically, wrote 'Why I Am What I Am' across the top of the page. Right away, since it came to mind as something characteristic of my personality, I began to write down a childhood memory of my shyness. Then, when I read what Hoja was writing about the wickedness of others, I had an idea which at that moment I believed to be important, and spoke up. Hoja should write about his own faults too. After reading what I'd written, he insisted that he was not a coward. I argued that though he wasn't a coward, he had his negative sides like everyone else, and if he delved into them he would find his true self. I had done this, and he

65

wanted to be like me; I could sense this in him. I saw him become angry when I said this, but he controlled himself and, trying to be rational, said that it was the others who were evil; not everyone, certainly, but it was because most people were imperfect and negative that everything was wrong in the world. At this I disagreed, saying that there was much in him that was wicked, even vile, and that he should recognize this. I added defiantly that he was worse than I was.

That was how those absurd and terrifying days of evil began! He'd tie me to the chair at my table and sit down facing me, ordering me to write what he wanted, though he no longer knew what this was. He had nothing in mind but that analogy: just as a person could view his external self in the mirror, he should be able to observe the interior of his mind in his thoughts. He said I knew how to do this but was withholding the secret from him. While Hoja sat across from me, waiting for me to write down this secret, I filled the sheets in front of me with stories exaggerating my own faults: I wrote with delight about the petty thefts of my childhood, the jealous lies, the way I schemed in order to make myself more loved than my brothers and sisters, the sexual indiscretions of my youth, stretching the truth more and more as I went along. The greedy curiosity with which Hoja read these tales, and the queer pleasure he derived from them, shocked me; afterwards he would become even more angry, intensifying the cruel treatment he had already let go beyond bounds. Perhaps it was because he could not tolerate the sins of a past he already sensed he would make his own. He began to beat me outright. After reading about one of my transgressions, he'd shout 'You rogue!' and bring his fist down upon my back with a vehemence that was only half in jest; once or twice, unable to control himself, he slapped me in the face. Perhaps he did these things because he was summoned even less frequently to the palace, because he had now convinced himself that he would find nothing to distract him other than the two of us, perhaps it was out of sheer frustration. But the more he read about my sins and increased his petty, infantile punishments, the more I became wrapped in a peculiar sense of security: for the first time, I began to think I had him in the palm of my hand.

Once, after he had hurt me very badly, I saw that he felt pity for me, but this was a malignant sentiment mixed with the repugnance felt for a person one doesn't consider in any way equal: I sensed this also in the way he was finally able to look at me without hatred. 'Let's not write any more,' he said. 'I don't want *you* to write any more,' he then corrected himself, for weeks had passed while he'd merely watched me write about my faults. He said we must leave this house, buried deeper in gloom with each passing day, and take a trip, perhaps to Gebze. He was going to turn once more to his work in astronomy, and he was thinking of writing a more rigorous treatise on the behaviour of ants. It alarmed me to see he was about to lose all respect for me, so in an effort to keep his interest I invented one more story that would expose my wickedness in the harshest light. Hoja read it with relish and did not even get angry; I sensed he merely felt intrigued at how I could abide being such an evil person. And perhaps, too, seeing such baseness, he no longer wanted to imitate me but was content to remain himself till the very end. Of course, he knew quite well that there was something of a game in all this. That day I spoke to him like a palace sycophant who knows he is not counted a real man; I tried to arouse his curiosity even more: what would he lose if, before leaving for Gebze, he tried one last time – in order to understand how I could be the way I was – to write about his own faults? What he wrote need not even be true, nor need anyone believe it. If he did this he would understand me and those like me, and one day this knowledge could be useful to him! Finally, unable to endure his own curiosity and my babbling, he said he would try it the following day. Of course, he didn't forget to add that he would do it only because he wanted to, not because he was taken in by my foolish games.

The next day was the most enjoyable of all those I spent in slavery. Although he didn't tie me to the chair, I spent the whole day sitting facing him so I could enjoy watching him become someone else. At first he believed so intensely in what he was doing that he didn't even bother to write that silly title of his, 'Why I Am What I Am', at the top of the page. He had the confident air of a mischievous child looking for an amusing lie; I could see at a glance that he was still within his own safe world. But this inflated sense of security didn't last long; neither did the show of contrition that he assumed for my sake. In a short time his pretended disdain became anxiety, the game became real; it bewildered and frightened him to act out this self-accusation, even if it were a pretence. He immediately crossed out what he wrote without showing it to me. But his curiosity had been aroused, and I believe he felt ashamed in front of me, for he persisted with it. Yet if he had followed his first impulse and got up from the table right away, perhaps he would not have lost his peace of mind.

During the next few hours I watched him slowly unravel: he'd write something critical about himself then tear it up without showing it to me, each time losing more of his self-confidence and self-respect, but then he'd begin again, hoping to recover what he'd lost. Supposedly he was going to show me his confessions; by nightfall I'd not seen one word of what I so longed to read, he'd ripped them all up and thrown them away, and his strength too was spent. When he shouted insults at me, saying this was a loathsome infidel's game, his self-confidence was at such a low ebb I even replied brazenly that he would get used to not feeling regret, to being evil. He got up and left the house, perhaps because he couldn't bear to be observed, and when he returned late I could tell from the perfume on him that, as I'd suspected, he'd been with prostitutes.

The next afternoon, to provoke him to continue working, I told Hoja he was surely strong enough not to be affected by such harmless games. Furthermore, we were doing this to learn something, not merely to pass the time, and in the end he would reach an understanding of why those he called fools were like that. Wasn't the prospect of really knowing one another fascinating enough? A man would be as spellbound by someone knowing the smallest details of his soul as he would by a nightmare.

It was not what I said, which he took about as seriously as he did the flattery of a palace dwarf, but the security of daylight that prompted him to sit down again at the table. When he got up that evening, he believed in himself even less than he had the day before. When I saw him set off to the prostitutes again that night, I pitied him.

Thus every morning he would sit down at the table, believing himself capable of transcending the evils he would write of that day and hoping to regain what he'd lost the day before, then every evening get up having left on the table a little more of what self-confidence he still had. Since he now found himself contemptible he could no longer look upon me with contempt; I thought I had at last found some confirmation of the equality I'd wrongly believed existed between us in the first days we'd spent together; this pleased me very much. Because he was wary of me, he said I needn't sit with him at the table; this too was a good sign, but my anger, gathering momentum for years, now grasped the bit between its teeth. I wanted to take revenge, to attack. Like him I had lost my balance. I felt that if I could make Hoja doubt himself just a little more, if I could read a few of those confessions he carefully kept from me and subtly humiliate him, then he would be the slave and sinner of the house, not I. There were already signs of this anyway: I could tell he needed now and then to be sure whether I was mocking him or not. He could no longer believe in himself, so had begun to seek my approval. He now asked my opinion more often on trivial daily affairs: were his clothes suitable, was the answer he'd given someone a good one, did I like his handwriting, what was I thinking? Not wanting him to despair completely and give up the game, I would sometimes criticize myself so as to raise his spirits. He'd give me that look that meant 'you rogue', but he no longer struck me; I was sure he thought he also deserved a beating.

I was extremely curious about these confessions that made him feel such self-hatred. Since I was accustomed to treating him as an inferior, even if only in secret, I thought they would consist of a few petty, insignificant sins. Now when I try to lend realism to my past, and tell myself to imagine in detail one or two of these confessions of which I never read one sentence, I somehow cannot find a sin Hoja could have committed that would destroy my story's consistency and the life I have imagined for myself. But I suppose that someone in my position can learn to trust himself again: I must say that I brought Hoja to make a discovery without his realizing it, that I exposed him to his own weak points and those of people like him, even if not entirely decisively and frankly. I probably thought the day was not far off when I would tell him and the others what I thought of them; I would destroy them by proving how wicked they were. I believe that those who read my story realize by now that I must have learned as much from Hoja as he learned from me! Maybe I just think this way now because when we are old we all look for more symmetry, even in the stories we read. I must have boiled over with a resentment gathering force for years. After Hoja had thoroughly humiliated himself I would make him accept my superiority, or at least my independence, and then derisively demand my freedom. I was dreaming that he would set me free without even grumbling, thinking of how I would write books about my adventures among the Turks when I returned to my country. How easy it had been for me to lose all sense of proportion! The news he brought me one morning suddenly changed all that.

Plague had broken out in the city! Since he said this as if speaking of some other, far away place, not of Istanbul, I didn't believe it at first; I asked how he'd heard the news, I wanted to know everything. The number of sudden deaths was rising for no apparent reason, presumably caused by some disease. I asked what the signs of illness were – perhaps it wasn't plague after all. Hoja laughed at me: I shouldn't worry, if I caught it I'd know beyond any doubt, a person had only three days of fever in which to find out. Some had swellings behind their ears, some under their armpits, on their bellies, buboes developed, then a fever took over; sometimes the boils burst, sometimes blood spewed from the lungs, there were those who died coughing violently like consumptives. He added that people from every district were dying in threes and fives. Anxious, I asked about our own neighbourhood. Hadn't I heard? A bricklayer who quarrelled with all the neighbours because their chickens were getting in through his wall, had died screaming with fever just one week ago. Only now did everyone realize that he'd died of the plague.

But I still didn't want to believe it; outside in the streets everything looked so normal, people passing by the window were so calm, I needed to find someone to share my alarm if I were to believe the plague was here. The next morning, when Hoja went to school, I flew out into the streets. I searched out the Italian converts I'd managed to meet during the eleven years I had spent here. One of them, known by his new name Mustafa Reis, had left for the dockyards; the other, Osman Efendi, wouldn't let me in at first although I knocked at his door as though I would beat it down with my fists. He had his servant say he wasn't at home but finally gave in and shouted after me. How could I still question whether the disease was real; didn't I see those coffins being carried down the street? He said I was scared, he could see it in my face, I was scared because I remained faithful to Christianity! He scolded me; a man must be a Muslim to be happy here, but he neglected to press my hand before he retreated into the dank darkness of his own house, didn't touch me at all. It was the hour of prayer, and when I saw the crowds in the courtyards of the mosques, I was seized with fear and started for home.

I was overcome by the bewilderment that strikes people at moments of disaster. It was as if I had lost my past, as though my memory had been drained, I was paralysed. When I saw a group carrying a funeral bier through the streets of our neighbourhood it completely unnerved me.

Hoja had come back from the school, I sensed he was pleased when he saw how I was. I noticed that my fear increased his self-confidence and this made me uneasy. I wanted him to be rid of this vain pride in his fearlessness. Trying to check my agitation, I poured out all my medical and literary knowledge; I described what I remembered from the scenes of plague in Hippocrates, Thucydides and Boccacio, said it was believed the disease was contagious, but this only made him more contemptuous – he didn't fear the plague; disease was God's will, if a man was fated to die he would die; for this reason it was useless to talk cowardly nonsense as I did about shutting oneself up in one's house and severing relations with the outside or trying to escape from Istanbul. If it was written, so it would come to pass, death would find us. Why was I afraid? Because of those sins of mine I'd written down day after day? He smiled, his eyes shining with certainty.

Until the day we lost one another I was never able to find out if he really believed what he said. Seeing him so completely undaunted I had been afraid for a moment, but then, when I remembered our discussions at the table, those terrifying games we played, I became sceptical. He was circling around, steering the conversation to the sins we'd written down together, reiterating the same idea with an air of conceit that drove me wild: if I was so afraid of death I couldn't have mastered the wickedness I appeared to write about so bravely. The courage I showed in pouring out my sins was simply the result of my shamelessness! Whereas he had hesitated at the time because he was so painstakingly attentive to the tiniest fault. But now he was calm, the deep confidence he felt in the face of the plague had left no doubt in his heart that he must be innocent.

Repelled by this explanation, which I stupidly believed, I decided to argue with him. Naïvely I suggested that he was confident not because he had a clear conscience but because he did not know that death was so near. I explained how we could protect ourselves from death, that we must not touch those who had caught the plague, that the corpses must be buried in limed pits, that people must reduce their contact with one another as much as possible, and that Hoja must not go to that crowded school.

It seems this last thing I said gave him ideas even more horrible than the plague. The next day at noon, saying he'd touched each of the children at school one by one, he stretched out his hands towards me; when he saw me balk, that I was afraid to touch him, he came closer and embraced me with glee; I wanted to scream, but like someone in a dream, I couldn't cry out. As for Hoja, he said, with a derisiveness I only learned to understand much later, that he was going to teach me fearlessness.

6

The plague was spreading quickly, but I somehow could not learn what Hoja called fearlessness. At the same time I wasn't as cautious as I had been at first. I could not stand any longer to be cooped up in one room like an ailing old woman, staring out the window for days on end. Once in a while I'd burst out into the street like a drunkard, watch the women shopping in the market-place, the tradesmen working in their shops, the men gathering in the coffee-houses after burying their dear ones, and try to learn to live with the plague. I might have done so, but Hoja would not leave me in peace.

Every night he'd reach for me with the hands he said he'd touched people with all day long. I'd wait without moving a muscle. You know how when, barely awake, you realize a scorpion is crawling over you and freeze, still as a statue – like that. His fingers did not resemble mine; running them coolly over my flesh Hoja would ask: 'Are you afraid?' I would not move. 'You're afraid. What are you afraid of?' Sometimes I'd feel an impulse to shove him away and fight, but I knew this would increase his rage even more. 'I'll tell you why you are afraid. You're afraid because you are guilty. You're afraid because you are steeped in sin. You're frightened because you believe in me more than I believe in you.'

And it was he who insisted we must sit down at the two ends of the table and write together. Now was the time to write why we were what we were. But again he ended up writing nothing more than why 'the others' were the way they were. For the first time he proudly showed me what he wrote. When I thought how he expected me to be humbled by what I read I could not hide my revulsion and told him he was no different from the fools he wrote about and that he would die before me.

I decided then that this prediction was my most effective weapon, and reminded him of his ten-years' labour, of the years he'd spent on theories of cosmography, the observations of the heavens he'd made at the expense of his eyesight, of the days he'd never taken his nose out of a book. Now it was I who would not leave him in peace; I said how foolish it would be for him to die in vain while it was possible to avoid the plague and go on living. By saying these things I increased not only his doubts but my punishments. I noticed then he seemed, as he read what I wrote, to grudgingly rediscover the respect for me he'd lost.

So as to forget my bad fortune in those days I filled page after page with the happy dreams I often had, not only at night, but during my midday naps as well. Trying to forget everything, as soon as I awoke I'd write down those dreams in which action and meaning were one, taking great pains to make my style poetic: I dreamt there were people living in the woods by our house who had solved the mysteries that for years we had wanted to understand, and if you dared to enter the darkness of the woods you became friends with them; our shadows were not extinguished with the setting of the sun, but took on a life of their own, mastering the thousand little things that we should have mastered while we slept peacefully in our clean, cool beds; the beautiful, three-dimensional people in the tableaux I fashioned in my dreams stepped out of their picture-frames and mingled among us; my mother, my father and I set up steel machines in our back garden to do our work for us...

Hoja was not unaware that these dreams were devilish traps that would drag him into the darkness of a deadly science, but still he continued to question me, realizing that he lost a bit more of his self-confidence with every question:

what did these silly dreams mean, did I really see them? Thus I first practised on him what we would do together years later with the sultan; I derived conclusions from our dreams about both of our futures: it was obvious that once infected by a fascination with science, a man could no more escape it than he could the plague; it wasn't hard to say that this addiction had taken hold of Hoja, but still I wondered about Hoja's dreams! He listened, openly mocking me, but since he had swallowed his pride to the extent of asking questions, he could not arouse my resentment much; and I could see that my answers aroused his curiosity. As I saw that the equanimity Hoja affected with the plague's appearance was being disturbed, my own fear of death did not diminish, but at least I no longer felt alone in my fear. Of course I paid the price of his nightly torments, but now I realized my struggle was not in vain: as he stretched out his hands toward me I told Hoja again that he would die before I did, and reminded him that those who were not afraid were ignorant, that his writings were left half-finished, that my dreams he'd read that day were full of happiness.

However, it wasn't what I said that brought matters to a head but something else. One day the father of a student of his at school came to the house. He seemed an innocuous, humble little man, said he lived in our neighbourhood. I listened, curled up in a corner like a sleepy house-cat, while they talked for a long time about this and that. Then our guest blurted out what he'd been dying to say: his cousin on his father's side had been left a widow last summer when her husband fell from the roof he was retiling. She now had many suitors, but our visitor had thought of Hoja because he'd heard from the neighbours that he was considering proposals of marriage. Hoja reacted more brutally than I'd expected: he said he did not want to marry, but even if he had he wouldn't take a widow. Upon this our visitor reminded us that the Prophet Muhammad had not minded Hadije's widowhood and even taken her as his first wife. Hoja said he'd heard of this widow, that she wasn't worth the saintly Hadije's little finger. Upon this our peculiar, proud neighbour wanted to make Hoja understand he himself was no prize either and said that although he didn't believe it, the neighbours were saying that Hoja had completely gone out of his mind, no one took as favourable signs all his stargazing, his playing with lenses and making strange clocks. With the spleen of a merchant criticizing the goods he intends to buy, our visitor added that the neighbours were saying that Hoja ate his food at a table like an infidel instead of sitting down cross-legged; that after paying purse upon purse of money for books, he threw them on the floor and trod on the pages in which the Prophet's name was written; that, unable to placate the devil within him by gazing at the sky for hours, he lay on his bed in broad daylight gazing at his dirty ceiling, took pleasure not in women but only young boys, I was his twin brother, he didn't fast during Ramadan and the plague had been sent on his account.

After he got rid of the visitor Hoja had a tantrum. I concluded that the complacency he derived from sharing the same attitudes that others held, or from pretending to do so, had come to an end. Wanting to deal him one last blow, I said that those who did not fear the plague were as stupid as this fellow. He became apprehensive, but asserted that he did not fear the plague either. Whatever the reason, I decided he had said this sincerely. He was extremely nervous, could not find anything to do with his hands, and kept repeating his refrain, lately forgotten, about the 'fools'. After nightfall he lit the lamp, placed it at the centre of the table, and said we would sit down. We must write.

Like two bachelors telling each other's fortunes to pass the time on endless winter nights, we sat at the table face to face, scratching out something or other on the empty pages before us. The absurdity of it! In the morning when I read what Hoja had written as his dream I found him even more ridiculous than I did myself. He had written down a dream in imitation of mine, but as everything about it made clear, this was a fantasy which had never been dreamt at all: he had us as brothers! He'd found it appropriate to play the role of elder to me while I listened obediently to his scientific lectures. The next morning as we ate breakfast he asked what I made of the neighbours' gossip about our being twins. This question pleased me but did not flatter my pride; I said nothing. Two days later he woke me up in the middle of the night to tell me that this time he had really dreamt that dream he wrote down. Perhaps it was true, but for some reason I didn't care. The next night he confessed he was afraid to die of plague.

Oppressed by being shut up in the house, I'd gone out into the streets at twilight: children were climbing trees in a garden and had left their colourful shoes on the ground; chattering women in line at the fountains no longer fell silent as I walked by; the market-places were full of shoppers; there were street brawls and people trying to break them up and others enjoying the spectacle. I tried to make myself believe that the epidemic had played itself out, but when I saw the coffins emerging one after another from the courtyard of the Beyazit Mosque I panicked and rushed home. As I entered my room Hoja called out: 'Come and have a look at this, will you.' His shirt unbuttoned, he was pointing to a small swelling, a red spot below his navel. 'There are so many insects around.' I came closer and looked carefully, it was a small red spot, slightly swollen, like a large insect bite, but why was he showing it to me? I was afraid to bring my face any nearer. 'An insect bite,' said Hoja, 'don't you think?' He touched the swelling with the tip of his finger. 'Or is it a flea bite?' I was silent, I didn't say I had never seen a flea bite like that.

I found some excuse to stay in the garden until sunset. I realized I must not stay in this house any longer, but I had no place in mind where I could go. And that spot really did look like an insect bite, it was not as prominent and broad as a plague bubo; but a little later my thoughts took another turn: perhaps because I was wandering in the garden among

78

the flourishing plants, it seemed to me that the red spot would swell up within two days, open like a flower, and burst, that Hoja would die, painfully. I told myself it might be an abscess caused by indigestion, but no, it looked like an insect bite, I thought I'd remember which insect it was in a moment, it had to be one of those huge nocturnal flying insects which thrive in tropical climates, but the name of the phantom-like creature would not even rise to the tip of my tongue.

When we sat down to dinner Hoja tried to pretend he was in good spirits, he joked, teased me, but he couldn't keep this up for long. Much later, after we had risen from the dinner we ate without speaking and the night, windless and silent, had settled in, Hoja said, 'I feel uneasy. My thoughts are heavy. Let's sit at the table and write.' Apparently this was the only way he could distract himself.

But he couldn't write. He sat idly watching me out of the corner of his eye while I wrote contentedly. 'What are you writing?' I read to him about how impatient I'd been returning home for vacation in a one-horse carriage after my first year of studies in engineering. But I had loved both the school and my friends; I read to him how I'd missed them while I sat alone on the bank of a stream reading the books I'd taken with me on vacation. After a short silence Hoja, as if revealing a secret, whispered suddenly: 'Do they always live happily like that there?' I thought he'd regret it as soon as he asked, but he was still looking at me with childish curiosity. I whispered too: 'I was happy!' A shadow of envy passed over his face, but it was not threatening. Shyly, haltingly, he told his story.

When he was twelve years old living in Edirne, there had been a period when he used to go with his mother and sister to the hospital of Beyazit Mosque to visit his mother's father who suffered from a stomach ailment. In the morning his mother would leave his brother, who was still too young to walk, at the neighbours, take Hoja, his sister, and a pot of pudding she'd prepared earlier, and they would set out together; the journey was short but delightful, along a road shaded with poplar trees. His grandfather would tell them stories. Hoja loved those stories, but loved the hospital more and would run off to wander through its courtyards and halls. On one visit he listened to music being played for the mental patients, under the lantern of a great dome; there was also the sound of water, flowing water; he'd wander through other rooms where strange, colourful bottles and jars shone brightly; another time he lost his way, started to cry, and they'd taken him to every room in the whole hospital one by one before finding his grandfather Abdullah Efendi's room; sometimes his mother cried, sometimes she listened with her daughter to the old man's stories. Then they'd leave with the empty pot grandfather had given back to them, but before they reached the house his mother would buy them halva and whisper, 'Let's eat it before anyone sees us.' They'd go to a secret place by a stream under the poplars where the three of them would sit with their toes dangling in the water, eating where no one could see them.

When Hoja finished talking a silence descended, making us uneasy while bringing us closer together with an unaccountable feeling of brotherhood. For a long time Hoja ignored the tension in the air. Later, after the heavy door of a nearby house was thoughtlessly slammed, he said he'd first felt his interest in science then, inspired by the patients and those colourful bottles, jars, and scales that brought them health. But after his grandfather died they did not go there again. Hoja had always dreamed he would grow up and return alone, but one year the Tunja River which flows through Edirne flooded without warning, the patients were removed from their beds, the rooms were filled with filthy, turbid water and when it finally receded that beautiful hospital remained buried for years under an accursed, stinking mud that could not be cleaned away.

As Hoja again fell silent our moment of intimacy was lost. He'd risen from the table, out of the corner of my eye

I saw his shadow pacing the room, then taking the lamp from the middle of the table he stepped behind me, and I could see neither Hoja nor his shadow; I wanted to turn around and look but didn't; it was as if I were afraid, expecting something evil. A moment later, hearing the rustle of clothes being taken off, I turned around apprehensively. He was standing in front of the mirror, naked from the waist up, carefully examining his chest and abdomen in the light of the lamp. 'My God,' he said, 'what kind of pustule is this?' I remained silent. 'Come and look at this, will you?' I didn't stir. He shouted, 'Come here, I say!' Fearfully I approached him like a student about to be punished.

I'd never been so close to his naked body; I didn't like it. At first I wanted to believe it was for this reason that I could not approach him, but I knew I was afraid of the pustule. He knew it as well. Yet, wanting to conceal my fear I brought my head near and muttered something, my eyes fixed upon that swelling, that inflammation, with the air of a doctor. 'You're afraid, aren't you?' Hoja said at last. Trying to prove that I was not, I brought my head even closer. 'You're afraid it's a plague bubo.' I pretended not to have heard, and was about to say an insect had bitten him, probably the same strange insect that bit me too once, somewhere, but the creature's name still did not come to mind. 'Touch it, will you!' said Hoja. 'Without touching it how will you know? Touch me!'

When he saw I wouldn't, he brightened up. He stretched out the fingers with which he'd touched the swelling towards my face. When he saw me start back with revulsion he laughed out loud, made fun of me for being afraid of a simple insect bite, but this merriment did not last long. 'I'm afraid to die,' he said suddenly. It was as if he were speaking of something else; he was more angry than ashamed; it was the anger of someone who felt betrayed. 'Don't you have a pustule like this? Are you sure? Take off your shirt, now!' At his insistence I pulled off my shirt like a child who hates to be washed. The room was hot, the window was shut,

81

but a cool breeze blew in from somewhere; perhaps it was the coldness of the mirror that made my flesh creep, I don't know. Ashamed of how I must look, I stepped outside of the mirror's frame. Now I saw Hoja's face reflected obliquely as he brought his head near my torso in the mirror; he'd bent that huge head everyone said resembled mine straight towards my body. He's doing this to poison my spirit, I thought all of a sudden; but I'd never done that to him, on the contrary, all these years I'd taken pride in being his teacher. Absurd as it was, for a moment I believed that bearded head, grotesque in the shadows of the lamplight, intended to suck my blood! Apparently I'd been much affected by those horror stories I'd loved to listen to as a child. While thinking this I felt his fingers on my abdomen; I wanted to run away, wanted to hit him over the head with something. 'You don't have one,' he said. He went behind me and examined my armpits, my neck, the backs of my ears. 'There are none here either, it seems the insect has not bitten you.'

Putting his hands on my shoulders he came forward and stood next to me. He acted like a dear old friend who had shared my deepest secrets. Squeezing the nape of my neck from both sides with his fingers, he pulled me towards him. 'Come, let us look in the mirror together.' I looked, and under the raw light of the lamp saw once more how much we resembled one another. I recalled how I'd been overwhelmed by this when I'd first seen him as I waited at Sadik Pasha's door. At that time I had seen someone I must be; and now I thought he too must be someone like me. The two of us were one person! This now seemed to me an obvious truth. It was as if I were bound fast, my hands tied, unable to budge. I made a movement to save myself, as if to verify that I was myself. I quickly ran my hands through my hair. But he imitated my gesture and did it perfectly, without disturbing the symmetry of the mirror image at all. He also imitated my look, the attitude of my head, he mimicked my terror I could not endure to see in the mirror but from which, transfixed by fear, I could not tear my eyes away; then he was gleeful like a child who teases a friend by mimicking his words and movements. He shouted that we would die together! What nonsense, I thought. But I was also afraid. It was the most terrifying of all the nights I spent with him.

Then he claimed he'd been afraid of the plague all along, everything he'd done had been done in order to test me, as when he'd watched Sadik Pasha's executioners lead me away to kill me, or when people had likened us to one another. Then he said he had taken possession of my spirit; just as a moment before he'd mirrored my movements, whatever I was thinking now, he knew it, and whatever I knew, he was thinking it! When he asked me what I was thinking at this moment, I couldn't think of anything but him and said I couldn't think of anything at all, but he wasn't listening to me, he was talking not to discover something but only to frighten me, to play upon his own fear, to make me share the burden of that fear. I sensed that the more he felt his loneliness the more he wanted to do me harm; as he ran his fingers over our faces, as he tried to bewitch me with the horror of that uncanny resemblance and himself grew even more excited and agitated than I was, I thought that he wanted to do something evil. I told myself that he kept holding me in front of the mirror, squeezing the nape of my neck, because his heart couldn't bear to commit this evil right away, but he seemed neither absurd nor helpless. He was right, I too wanted to say and do the things he said and did, I envied him because he could take action when I could not, because he could play upon the fear in the plague and the mirror.

But despite the intensity of my fear, although I believed I'd just seen things about myself I'd never noticed before, I somehow could not shake off the feeling that it was all a game. His fingers on my neck had relaxed, but I did not step out of the frame of the mirror. 'Now I am like you,' he said. 'I know your fear. I have become you!' I understood what he was saying but tried to convince myself that this prophecy, half of which I now have no doubt is true, was silly and childish. He claimed he could see the world as I did; 'they', he was saying again, now at last he understood how 'they' thought, how 'they' felt. Letting his gaze wander beyond the mirror-frame, he talked for a while, glancing around in the shadows at the table, the glasses, the chairs and objects half illuminated by the lamplight. He declared he could now say things he couldn't before because he had not been able to see them, but I thought he was mistaken: the words were the same, and so were the objects. The only thing new was his fear; no, not that either; the form of his experience of it; but it seemed to me that even this, which I cannot clearly describe now, was something he put on in front of the mirror, a new trick of his. And unwillingly putting aside this game too, his mind seemed to whirl back to dwell upon that red pustule, asking: was it an insect or was it plague?

He spoke for a while about how he wanted to pick up from where I had left off. We were still standing half-naked in front of the mirror. He was going to take my place, I his, and to accomplish this it would be enough for us to exchange clothes and for him to cut his beard while I left mine to grow. This thought made our resemblance in the mirror even more horrible, and my nerves grew taut as I heard him say that I would then make a freedman of him: he spoke exultantly of what he would do when he returned to my country in my place. I was terrified to realize he remembered everything I had told him about my childhood and youth, down to the smallest detail, and from these details had constructed an odd and fantastical land to his own taste. My life was beyond my control, it was being dragged elsewhere in his hands, and I felt there was nothing for me to do but passively watch what happened to me from the outside, as if I were dreaming. But the trip he was going to take to my country as me and the life he was going to live there had a strangeness and naïveté that prevented me from believing it completely. At the same time I was surprised by the logic in the details of his fantasy: I felt like saying that this too could have been, my life could have been lived like this. Then I understood I'd sensed something more profound about Hoja's life for the first time, but wasn't able to say what this was just yet. All I could do, as I listened in confusion to what 'I' would do in my old world I'd longed for all these years, was to forget the fear of plague.

But this didn't last long. Hoja now wanted me to say what I would do when I took his place. My nerves were so exhausted from holding myself rigid in that bizarre pose, trying to believe we didn't look alike and that the swelling was only an insect bite, that nothing at all came to mind. When he insisted, I remembered I'd once planned to write my memoirs when I returned to my country: when I said I might one day make a good story of his adventures, he looked at me in disgust. I didn't know him as well as he knew me – in fact not at all! Shoving me out of the way, he stood alone in front of the mirror: when he took my place he would decide what would happen to me! He said the swelling was a plague bubo; I was going to die. He described how horribly I would suffer before I died; the fear, for which I was unprepared since I had not yet realized it would come, would be worse than death. While he was saying how I would be strangled by the torments of the disease, Hoja had stepped out of the mirror's frame; when I looked again he was stretched out on his bed that he had rolled out untidily on the floor, describing the torments I would suffer. His hand was on his belly, as if, it occurred to me, to touch the pain he was describing. Just then he called out, and when I, trembling, went to his side, I immediately regretted it; he tried to lay his hand on me again. Whatever the reason, I now thought it was just an insect bite, but still I was afraid.

The whole night passed like this. While he tried to infect me with the disease and the fear of it, he kept repeating that I was he and he was I. He's doing this because he enjoys going outside himself, observing himself from a distance, I thought, and kept on repeating to myself, like someone struggling to awake from a dream: it's a game; for he was using this word 'game' himself, but he was sweating heavily like someone physically ill rather than like a person suffocated by malignant thoughts in a hot room.

As the sun rose he was talking about stars and death, about his false predictions, the sultan's stupidity and worse, his ingratitude, about his own beloved fools, 'us' and 'them', about how he wanted to be someone else. I wasn't listening anymore, I went out into the garden. For some reason my mind was preoccupied with the ideas about immortality I'd read of in an ancient book. There was no movement outside other than that of the sparrows chirping and fluttering from branch to branch among the linden trees. How bewildering was the stillness! I thought of other rooms in Istanbul where victims of the plague lay dying. If Hoja's illness was plague it would go on like this till he died, I reflected, and if not, until that red swelling disappeared. By now I had realized I wouldn't be able to stay in this house much longer. When I went inside I had no idea where I could escape to, where I would hide. I was dreaming of a place far from Hoja, far from the plague. As I stuffed a few pieces of my clothing into a bag, I only knew this place must be near enough for me to reach without being caught.

7

I had put aside a little money by stealing a bit from Hoja whenever I could, and had some I'd earned here and there. Before I left the house I took this money from the chest where I'd hidden it in a sock among the books he now never looked at. Seized by curiosity, I then went into Hoja's room, where he had fallen asleep, sweating profusely, with the lamp burning. I was surprised by how small the mirror was which had terrified me all night long with that bewitching resemblance I had never been able completely to believe in. Without touching anything, I left the house in a hurry. A light breeze blew as I walked down the empty streets of the neighbourhood. I had an impulse to wash my hands, I knew where I would go, I was content. I was enjoying walking in the streets in the silence of dawn, descending the hills towards the sea, washing my hands at the fountains, taking in the view of the Golden Horn.

I'd first heard of Heybeli Island from a young monk who'd come to Istanbul from there; when we met in the European quarter of Galata he had enthusiastically described the beauty of the islands. It must have made an impression on me, for as I left our district I knew it was there I would go. The ferrymen and fishermen I spoke with wanted incredible amounts of money to take me to the island, and I became depressed thinking they knew I was a runaway – they'll betray me to the men Hoja will send after me! Later I decided this was how they intimidated the Christians they looked down on for being afraid of the plague. Trying not to attract attention, I struck a bargain with the second boatman I spoke with. He was not a strong man, and he spent less effort on rowing than he did on talking about the plague and the sins which it had been sent to punish. For good measure he added that it was no use trying to escape the plague by taking refuge on the island. As he talked I realized he must have been as afraid as I was. The journey took six hours.

It was only later that I thought of my days on the island as happy. I paid little to stay in the home of a lone Greek fisherman, and tried to keep out of sight for I did not feel altogether safe. Sometimes I'd think that Hoja was dead, sometimes that he would send men after me. On the island there were many Christians like me fleeing the plague, but I didn't want them to notice me.

I'd go to sea with the fisherman every morning and return in the evening. For a while I took up spearing lobster and crab. If the weather was too bad for fishing I'd walk around the island, and there were times when I'd go to the garden of the monastery and sleep peacefully under the vines. There was one bower supported by a fig-tree from which you could see as far as Hagia Sofia in fine weather, where I'd sit in the shade gazing at Istanbul, daydreaming for hours on end. In one dream I was sailing to the island and saw Hoja among the dolphins swimming alongside the boat, he'd made friends with them and was asking about me; another time my mother was with them and they scolded me for being late. When I woke up sweating with the sun on my face I'd want to return to these dreams, but unable to, I'd force myself to think: sometimes I'd imagine that Hoja had died and I could see the dead body inside the empty house I'd abandoned, I could feel the silence of the funeral which no one would come to; then I'd think of his predictions, of the amusing things he'd invented happily as well as those he'd concocted in disgust and rage; of the sultan and his animals. Accompanying these day-dreams with the heavy dancing of their claws were the lobsters and crabs I speared through their backs.

I tried to convince myself that sooner or later I would be able to escape to my own country. I only had to steal from the open doors on the island, but before that it was essential that I forget Hoja. For I had fallen unawares under the spell of what had happened to me, of the temptation of memory; I could almost blame myself for abandoning a man who looked so much like me. Just as I do now, I longed for him passionately; did he actually resemble me as much as he did in memory or was I fooling myself? It was as though I'd not once really looked into his face in these eleven years; in fact I'd often done so. I even felt the urge to go to Istanbul and see his corpse one last time. I decided that if I were to be free I must convince myself that the uncanny resemblance between us was a blunder of memory, a bitter illusion that should be forgotten, and I must get used to this fact.

Luckily I did not get used to it. For one day I suddenly saw Hoja before me. I had stretched out in the fisherman's backyard daydreaming, my closed eyes turned towards the sun, when I felt his shadow. He was facing me, smiling like someone who loved me rather than someone who'd beaten me in a game. I had an extraordinary feeling of security, so much that it alarmed me. Perhaps I had secretly been waiting for this, for I immediately retreated into the guilty feelings of a lazy slave, a humble, bowing servant. While I gathered my things together, instead of hating Hoja I reviled myself. And it was he who paid my debt to the fisherman. He'd brought two men with him and we returned swiftly with double oars. We were home before nightfall. I'd missed the smell of home. And the mirror had been taken down from the wall.

The next morning Hoja confronted me: my crime was very serious and he was burning to punish me, not only for running away but because I'd abandoned him on his deathbed believing an insect bite was a plague bubo, but now was not the time. He explained that the previous week the sultan had finally called for him and asked when this plague would end, how many more lives it would take, whether or not his own life was in danger. Hoja, very excited, had given evasive answers because he wasn't prepared, and had begged for time saying he needed to work from the stars. He'd danced home wild with victory, but wasn't sure how to manipulate the sultan's interest to his own advantage. So he had decided to bring me back.

He'd known for a long time that I was on the island; after I'd run away he'd gone down with a cold, gone after me three days later, picked up my trail from the fishermen, and when he opened his purse a little the talkative boatman revealed he'd taken me to Heybeli. Since Hoja knew I could not escape further than the islands, he hadn't followed me. When he said this meeting with the sultan was the crucial opportunity of his life I agreed with him. And he said frankly that he had need of my knowledge.

We began work immediately. Hoja had the decisive air of a man who knows what he wants; I was delighted at this sense of determination I had rarely observed in him before. Since we knew he would be called again the next day we decided to stall for time. We agreed at once that we should not give much information and mention only what was likely to be confirmed. Hoja's acuity, which I so admired, had brought him straightaway to the opinion 'prediction is buffoonery, but it can be well used to influence fools'. As he listened to me talk he seemed to agree the plague was a disaster which could only be arrested by health precautions. Like me he did not deny that the disaster was God's will, but only indirectly; for this reason even we mortals could take stock and act to protect ourselves without offending God's pride. Hadn't the Caliph Omar the Rightly Guided recalled General Ebu Ubeyde from Syria to Medina in order to protect his army from the plague? Hoja would ask the sultan to reduce his contacts with others to an absolute minimum for his own protection. It was not that we didn't think of persuading the sovereign to take these precautions by putting the fear of death in his heart, but this was dangerous. It was not simply a matter of frightening the sultan with a rhetorical description of death; even if Hoja's chattering impressed him, he had a crowd of fools around him to share his fear and help him conquer it; later these unscrupulous fools could always accuse Hoja of irreligion. So, relying on my knowledge of literature, we concocted a tale to tell the sultan.

The thing that most daunted Hoja was how to decide when the plague might end. I realized that we had to start from the figures of the daily death-toll; when I told Hoja this he didn't seem very impressed, he agreed to ask the sultan for help in obtaining these figures but would mask the real intention of his request. I am not a great believer in mathematics, but our hands were tied.

The next morning he went to the palace, and I into the plague-stricken city. I was just as afraid of the plague as before, but the raucous movement of ordinary life, the ubiquitous desire to gain something of the world, even if only some small share, made my head spin. It was a cool, breezy summer day; as I wandered among the dead and the dying I thought how it had been years since I had been able to love life this much. I went into the mosque courtyards, wrote down the number of coffins on a piece of paper, and walking through the various neighbourhoods, tried to establish a relationship between what I saw and the death-count: it was not easy to find a meaning in all the houses, the people, the crowds, the gaiety and sorrow and joy. And oddly enough my eye hungered only for the details, the lives of others, the happiness, helplessness, indifference of people living in their own homes with their own families and friends.

Towards noon I crossed over to the other shore of the Golden Horn, to the European quarter of Galata, and intoxicated by the crowds and the corpses I wandered through poor coffee-houses, around the dockyards, shyly smoked tobacco, ate in a humble cookshop simply out of a desire to understand, strolled in bazaars and stores. I wanted to engrave every single detail on my mind so I could reach some sort of conclusion. I returned home after twilight, exhausted, and listened to Hoja's news from the palace.

Things had gone well. The story we invented had affected the sultan deeply. His mind accepted the idea that the plague was like a devil trying to deceive him by taking on human form; he decided not to allow strangers into the palace; comings and goings were kept under strict supervision. When Hoja was asked when and how the plague would end, he had talked up such a storm that the sultan said fearfully that he could see Azrael, the angel of death, wandering the city like a drunkard; he'd take by the hand whoever he fixed his eye on and drag him away. Hoja was quick to correct him, it was not Azrael but Satan who lured men to their deaths: and he wasn't drunk but extremely cunning. Hoja, as we planned, had made clear that it was imperative to make war on Satan. To understand when the plague would leave the city in peace, it was crucial to observe its movements. Although among his retinue there were those who said that to make war on the plague was to oppose God, the sultan paid no attention; and later he asked about his animals; would the plague-devil harm his falcons, his hawks, his lions, his monkeys? Hoja had immediately replied that the devil came to men in the form of a man and to animals in the form of a mouse. The sultan ordered that five hundred cats be brought from a far away city untouched by plague, and that Hoja be given as many men as he wanted.

Straightaway we scattered the twelve men given to our command to the four corners of Istanbul to patrol every district and report to us the death-count and whatever else they observed. We'd spread out on our table a rough map of Istanbul I had drawn, copied from books. With dread and delight, at night we marked on the map where the plague had spread, outlining the results we would present to the sultan.

We were not optimistic at first. The plague was roving the city like an aimless vagabond, not a cunning devil. One day it took forty lives in the district of Aksaray, the next day struck Fatih, appeared suddenly on the other shore, in Tophane, Jihangir, and the following day when we looked again it had barely touched those places and after passing through Zeyrek entered our district overlooking the Golden Horn, taking twenty lives. We could understand nothing from the death-tolls; one day five hundred went, the next day one hundred. We wasted much time before realizing we needed to know not where the plague killed its victims but where the infection was first caught. The sultan was calling for Hoja again. We thought it over carefully and decided he should say the plague roved in crowded market-places, in the bazaars where people cheated each other, the coffee-houses where they sat down close to one another and gossiped. He left, returning in the evening.

Hoja had told him. 'What shall we do?' the sultan had asked. Hoja advised that the to and fro in the market-places and the city be reduced by physical force: the simpletons around the sovereign opposed this immediately, of course: how would the city be fed, if business stopped life also stopped, news of a plague wandering in the form of a man would terrify those who heard of it, they would believe the Day of Judgement had come and would grab the bit between their teeth; no one wanted to be imprisoned in a neighbourhood where the plague devil roamed, they would raise a rebellion. 'And they are right,' said Hoja. At that moment some fool had asked where one would find enough men to control the populace to this degree, and the sultan became furious; he frightened everyone by saying he'd punish anyone who doubted his power. In his rage he ordered that Hoja's recommendations be carried out, but not without consulting his circle first. The Imperial Astrologer Sitki Efendi, whose teeth were sharp where Hoja was concerned, reminded him that he still had not said when the plague would leave Istanbul. Afraid the sultan would defer to him, Hoja said he would bring a calendar on his next visit.

We had filled the map on the table with marks and figures,

but we hadn't found any logic in the plague's movements about the city. By now the sultan had put the recommended prohibitions in force and they had been observed for more than three days. Janissaries guarded the entrances to the market-places, the avenues, the boat landings, halting passers-by, interrogating them: 'Who are you? Where are you going? Where are you coming from?' They sent the timid, surprised travellers and idlers back to their homes so that they should not be taken in by the plague. By the time we learned that activity had slowed in the Grand Bazaar and Unkapi, we were pondering the death-toll figures we'd collected the past month, written on scraps of paper and pinned up on the wall. In Hoja's opinion we were waiting in vain for the plague to move according to some logic and if we were to save our heads we must invent something to put the sultan off.

It was around this time too that the permit system was instituted. The Aga of the Janissaries distributed permits to those whose work was considered essential for commerce to continue and the city to be fed. When I was beginning to see a pattern in the death-counts for the first time, we learned the Aga was collecting a great deal of money from this, and that the small tradesmen, unwilling to pay, had begun preparations for a rebellion. While Hoja was saying the Grand Vizier Koprulu planned to mount a conspiracy in league with the small tradesmen, I interrupted him to tell him about the pattern and tried to make him believe the plague had slowly withdrawn from the outer neigh-bourhoods and poor districts.

What I said did not quite convince him, but he left the work of preparing the calendar to me. He said he'd written a story to distract the sultan which was so meaningless that no one would be able to conclude anything from it. A few days later he asked if it were possible to make up a story that had no moral or meaning other than the pleasure of reading or listening to it. 'Like music?' I suggested, and Hoja looked surprised. We discussed how the ideal story should begin innocently like a fairy-tale, be frightening like a nightmare in the middle, and conclude sadly like a love story ending in separation. The night before he went to the palace we sat up chattering happily, working in haste. In the next room our left-handed calligrapher friend was writing out a clean copy of the beginning of the story Hoja had still not managed to finish. Towards morning, working with the limited figures I had in hand, I had concluded from the equations I'd struggled for days to produce that the plague would take its last victims in the markets and leave the city in twenty days. Hoja didn't ask me what I based this conclusion on, and remarking only that the day of salvation was too far off he told me to revise the calendar for a two-week period and conceal the duration with other figures. I doubted this would succeed, but I did what he said. Hoja then and there composed verse chronograms for some of the dates and thrust them into the hand of the calligrapher who was just about to finish his work; he told me to draw pictures illustrating some of the verses. Towards noon, irritable, depressed, and frightened, he hurriedly bound the treatise with a blue marbled cover and left with it. He said he had less faith in the calendar than in those pelicans, winged bulls, red ants and talking monkeys he'd crammed into his story.

When he returned in the evening he was exhilarated, and this exuberance dominated the three weeks during which he completely convinced the sultan of the soundness of his prediction: at the beginning he'd said, 'Anything can happen', the first day he was not at all hopeful; a few in the crowd gathered around the sultan had even laughed while listening to his story recited by a youth with a beautiful voice. Of course they did this on purpose to belittle Hoja, to put him out of favour with the sultan, but the sovereign demanded silence and reprimanded them; he asked Hoja only on what signs he had based his conclusion that the plague would end in two weeks. Hoja replied that everything was contained in the story, which no one had been able to understand. Then, in order to please the sultan, he'd made a show of affection for the cats of every colour brought by ship from Trabzon which were now swarming over the inner courtyards and into every room of the palace.

He said that by the time he had arrived on the second day the palace was divided into two camps; one group, which included the Imperial Astrologer Sitki Efendi, wanted to lift all the precautions imposed on the city; the others taking Hoja's part said, 'Let the city not even breathe, let it not inhale the plague devil roving within.' I was hopeful as I watched the death-counts fall day by day, but Hoja was still anxious, it was whispered that the first group, reaching an understanding with Koprulu, had begun preparations for a revolt; their goal was not to conquer the plague but to be free of their rivals.

At the end of the first week there was a visible reduction in the number of deaths, but my calculations showed that the epidemic would not disappear in just one more week. I grumbled at Hoja for changing my calendar, but now he was hopeful; he told me excitedly that the whisperings about the grand vizier had ceased. On top of this Hoja's party had spread the news that Koprulu was collaborating with them. As for the sultan, he was thoroughly frightened by all these machinations and sought peace of mind with his cats.

As the second week came to an end the city was suffocating more from the precautions than from the plague; with each passing day fewer people died, but only we and those who like us followed the death-counts realized this. Rumours of famine had broken out, mighty Istanbul was like an abandoned city; Hoja told me about it, for I never left the neighbourhood: a man could feel the desperation of people being strangled by plague behind all those closed windows and courtyard gates, waiting for some reprieve from plague and death. The palace too was in a state of suspense, every time a cup fell on the floor or someone coughed loudly, that crowd of wiseacres burst their bladders in anticipation, whispering all at once 'Let us see what decision the sultan will make today', hysterical like all help-less souls who yearn for something to happen, whatever it might be. Hoja was swept away by this agitation; he'd tried to explain to the sultan that the plague had gradually with-drawn, that his predictions had proved correct, but he hadn't been able to make much of an impression on him, and in the end was forced again to talk about animals.

Two days later he'd been able to conclude from a count made at the mosques that the epidemic had thoroughly receded, but Hoja's happiness that Friday was due more to the fact that a group among the despairing tradesmen had clashed with the janissaries guarding the roads, and that another group of janissaries discontented with the preven-tive measures had joined forces with a couple of idiot imams preaching in the mosques, some vagrants eager for loot and other idlers who said the plague was God's will and no one should interfere with it. But this turmoil was suppressed before it got out of hand. When a judgement was obtained from the sheikh of Islam, twenty men were executed immediately, perhaps to make these events seem more momentous than they were. Hoja was delighted.

The following evening he announced his victory. No longer could anyone in the palace complain that the preven-tive measures should be lifted; when the Aga of the Janis-saries was summoned, he'd made mention of the rebel par-tisans in the palace; the sultan had been angered; that group whose enmities had for a while made life hard for Hoja, scattered like a covey of partridges. For a time it was whis-pered that Koprulu would take harsh measures against the rebels with whom it was believed he had collaborated. Hoja announced with evident pleasure that he'd influenced the sultan in this regard as well. Those who put down the revolt had been trying to convince the sultan that the plague had subsided. And what they said was true. The sovereign praised Hoja as he'd never done before; he took him to see the monkeys he'd had brought from Africa in a cage made specially to his order. While they watched the monkeys, whose filth and impertinence disgusted Hoja, the sovereign asked whether they could learn to speak like parrots could. Turning towards his retinue the sultan had declared that in future he wanted to see Hoja at his side more often, the calendar he'd devised had proved correct.

One Friday a month later Hoja was appointed Imperial Astrologer; he became even more than that: as the sultan went to the Hagia Sophia Mosque for the Friday prayers in which the entire city participated to celebrate the end of the plague, Hoja followed directly behind him; the precautions had been lifted, and I too was among the cheering crowds giving thanks to God and the sultan. While the sovereign passed before us on horseback, the populace screamed with all their might; they became ecstatic, there was pushing and shoving, the crowd rose up in a wave and the janissaries pushed us back, for a moment I was squeezed against a tree by the people who surged over me, and when, elbowing the crowd, I threw myself to the front, I came face to face with Hoja, walking four or five steps away from me looking pleased and happy. He glanced away as if he didn't know me. In that incredible uproar, suddenly, stupidly swept up in the general enthusiasm, I believed Hoja had not seen me at that moment, that if I shouted out to him with all my strength he would be made aware of my existence and rescue me from the crowd, and I would join that happy parade of those who held the reins of victory and power! It wasn't that I wished to seize a share in the triumph or to receive a reward for what I had done; the feeling I had was quite different: I should be by his side, I was Hoja's very self! I had become separated from my real self and was seeing myself from the outside, just as in the nightmares I often had. I didn't even want to learn the identity of this other person I was inside of; I only wanted, while I fearfully watched my self pass by without recognizing me, to rejoin him as soon as I could. But a brute of a soldier pushed me back with all his strength into the crowd.

8

In the weeks after the plague subsided Hoja was not only
raised to the position of imperial astrologer, but also
developed a more intimate relationship with the sultan than
we had ever hoped for: the grand vizier, after the failure of
that minor uprising, persuaded the sovereign's mother that
her son should now be rescued from those buffoons he kept
around him; for both the tradesmen and the janissaries held
that crowd of wiseacres, who misled the sultan with their
idle nonsense, responsible for the troubles. So when the
faction of the former Imperial Astrologer Sitki Efendi, who
was said to have had a hand in the plot, was driven from
the palace into exile or a change of position, their duties
were left to Hoja as well.

By now he was going every day to one of the palaces
where the sultan was in residence, conversing with him
during hours the sultan regularly set aside for their talks.
When Hoja returned home he'd tell me, elated and trium-
phant, how every morning the sultan would first of all have
him interpret his dream of the night before. Of all the func-
tions Hoja had assumed he perhaps loved this one most: when
the sultan admitted sadly one morning that he'd had no
dream the night before, Hoja proposed he interpret someone else's dream, and when the sovereign enthusiastically
accepted this, the imperial guards rushed to find someone
who'd had a good dream and brought him into the sovereign's
presence, and thus it became an abiding custom that a dream
be interpreted every morning. The rest of the time, as they
strolled through the gardens shaded by flowering erguvan

and great plane-trees, or sailed the Bosphorus in caiques, they would talk of the sultan's beloved animals and, of course, the creatures we had imagined. But he was broaching other subjects with the sultan as well, which he exuberantly recounted to me: what was the cause of the Bosphorus currents? What valuable knowledge could be learned from observing the methodical habits of ants? From whence did the magnet derive its power, other than from God? What significance was there in the hither and thither of the stars? Could anything be found in the customs of infidels but infidelity, anything that was worth knowing? Could one invent a weapon that would scatter their armies in fear and dread? After telling me how attentively the sultan had listened to him, Hoja would dash to the table and draw designs on expensive, heavy paper for the weapon: long-barrelled cannon, firing mechanisms that detonated by themselves, engines of war, apparitions making one think of satanic beasts, calling me to the table to bear witness to the violence of these images he said would very soon be realized.

Yet I wanted to share in these dreams with Hoja. Perhaps this was why my mind still lingered on the plague that had made us experience those dreadful days of brotherhood. All Istanbul had prayed at Hagia Sophia in thanks for deliverance from the plague-devil, but the disease had still not completely withdrawn from the city. In the mornings, while Hoja hurried to the sultan's palace, I wandered the city anxiously, keeping count of the funerals still taking place in the neighbourhood mosques with their squat minarets, the poor little mosques with red-tiled roofs overgrown with moss, hoping out of motives I could not understand, that the disease would not leave the city and us.

While Hoja talked of how he had influenced the sultan, of his victory, I would explain to him that the epidemic was still not over and that since the preventive restrictions had been lifted it could flare up anew any day. He would silence me angrily, claiming I was jealous of his triumph. I saw his point: he was now imperial astrologer, the sultan told him his dreams every morning, he could make the sultan listen to him in private without that whole crowd of fools around, these were things we'd waited fifteen years for, it was a victory; but why did he speak as if the victory were his alone? He seemed to have forgotten that it was I who had proposed the measures against the plague, I who had prepared the calendar that didn't quite prove accurate but had been received as if it were; what I resented even more was that he remembered only that I'd fled to the island, not the circumstances under which he'd hurriedly brought me back.

Perhaps he was right, perhaps what I felt could be called jealousy, but what he didn't realize was that this was a fraternal feeling. I wanted him to understand this, but when I made him recall how in the days before the plague we used to sit at the two ends of a table like two bachelors trying to forget the boredom of lonely nights, when I reminded him of how sometimes he or I had been afraid but we had learned so much from these fears, and confessed that I had missed those nights even while I was alone on the island, he listened contemptuously to everything I said as if he were merely a witness to my hypocrisy surfacing in a game he himself took no part in, he gave me no hope, he said nothing to hint that we would return to those days when we lived together as brothers.

As I wandered from district to district I could now see that, despite the lifting of restrictions, the plague, as if it didn't want to cast a shadow over this thing Hoja called 'victory', was slowly receding from the city. Sometimes I wondered why it made me lonely to think the dark fear of death was withdrawing from our midst and going away. Sometimes I wanted us to talk, not about the sultan's dreams or the projects Hoja described to him, but about our earlier days together: I'd long been ready to stand together with him, even with the fear of death, and face the dreadful mirror he'd taken down from the wall. But for a long time now Hoja had been treating me with contempt, or pretending to; what's worse, at times I believed he could not be bothered to do even that.

Now and then, trying to draw him back to our former happy life, I'd say the time had come for us to sit down at the table again. So as to set an example, I tried once or twice to write; when I read him the pages I'd filled with exaggerated accounts of the terror of plague, of that desire to do evil born of fear, of my sins left half-told, he didn't even listen to me. He said mockingly, with a force he perhaps derived more from my helplessness than from his own triumph, that he'd realized even then that our writings were nothing but nonsense, at the time he'd played those games out of boredom, just to see where they would end, and because he'd wanted to test me: in any case he'd known what kind of man I was the day I ran away believing he'd been infected by the plague. I was an evil-doer! There were two types of men; the righteous like him and the guilty like me.

I made no reply to these words of his, which I tried to attribute to the intoxication of victory. My mind was as sharp as ever, and when I caught myself becoming angry at trivialities I knew I had not lost my ability to feel rage, but I seemed not to know how to respond to his provocations, nor how to lead him on, how to catch him in a trap. During the days I spent in flight from him on Heybeli Island I realized that I had lost sight of my goal. What difference would it make if I returned to Venice? After fifteen years my mind had long accepted that my mother had died, my fiancée was lost to me, married, with a family; I didn't want to think of them, they appeared less and less in my dreams; moreover I no longer saw myself among them in Venice as in my first years, but dreamt of their living in Istanbul, in our midst. I knew that if I should return to Venice I would not be able to pick up my life where I'd left it. At most I might be able to begin anew with another life. I no longer felt any enthusiasm for the details of that previous life, unless for the sake of one or two books I'd once planned to write about the Turks and my years of slavery.

Sometimes I thought Hoja treated me with contempt because he sensed I had no country and no purpose, because he knew I was weak, and sometimes I doubted he understood even this much. Each day he was so intoxicated by the stories he'd told the sultan, by the image and the triumph of that incredible weapon he dreamed about and said would definitely win over the sultan, that perhaps he did not even realize what I was thinking. I'd catch myself observing this totally self-absorbed contentment of Hoja's with envy. I loved him, I loved that false exhilaration he got from his exaggerated sense of victory, his never-ending plans, and the way he said he'd soon have the sultan in the palm of his hand. I couldn't have admitted, even to myself, that I had thoughts like these, but while I followed his movements, his daily actions, I was sometimes overcome by the feeling that I was watching myself. Looking at a child, a youth, a man will sometimes see his own childhood and youth and observe him with love and curiosity: the fear and curiosity I felt was of that kind; it often came back to me how he had grasped the nape of my neck and said, 'I have become you', but when I reminded him of those days, Hoja would cut me short and talk about what he had said that day to the sultan to make him believe in the unbelievable weapon, or describe in detail how that morning he had seduced the sovereign's mind while interpreting his dream.

I, too, wanted to be able to believe in the brilliance of these successes he made sound so sweet as he recounted them. Sometimes it happened that, carried away by my boundless fantasies, I gladly put myself in his place and did believe in them. Then I would love him and myself, us, and with my mouth hanging open like a simpleton listening to an engrossing fairy-tale, lost in what he was saying, I'd believe that he spoke of those wonderful days to come as a goal we would pursue together.

This was how I came to join him in interpreting the sultan's dreams. Hoja had decided to provoke the twenty-one-year-old sovereign to assert greater control over the government.

Thus he explained to him that the lone horses the sultan often saw galloping wildly in his dreams were sad because they were riderless; and that the wolves who sank their merciless teeth into their quarries' throats were happy because they were self-sufficient; that the weeping old women and beautiful blind girls and the trees whose leaves were stripped off in black rains were calling out to him for help; that the sacred spiders and the proud falcons symbolized the virtues of independence. We wanted the sultan to be interested in our science after he took control of the government; we even exploited his nightmares towards this end. During the long, exhausting nights on hunting excursions the sultan, like most who love the hunt, would dream that he himself was the prey, or, in his fear of losing the throne, that he saw himself sitting on the throne as a child, and Hoja would explain that on the throne he would remain forever young, but only by making weapons superior to those of our ever-vigilant enemies could he be safe from their treachery. The sultan dreamt that his grandfather Sultan Murat had proved his strength by striking a donkey in two with a single blow of his sword so swiftly that its two halves galloped away from one another; that the shrew called Kosem Sultana, his grandmother, rose from the grave to strangle him and his mother, and leapt upon him stark naked; that instead of the plane-trees in the hippodrome, there grew fig-trees from which bloody corpses dangled instead of fruit; that evil men whose faces resembled his own were chasing him in order to thrust him into the sacks they carried and smother him; or that an army of turtles with candles on their backs whose flames were somehow not blown out by the wind, entered the sea from Uskudar and was marching straight for the palace, and we tried to interpret these dreams, which I patiently and cheerfully wrote down in a book and classified, to the advantage of science and the incredible weapon which must be built, thinking how wrong were the courtiers who whispered that the sultan neglected the affairs of government and had nothing in his head but hunting and animals.

According to Hoja we were gradually influencing him, but I no longer believed we would succeed. Hoja would obtain his promise regarding a new weapon or the establishment of an observatory or a house of sciences, and after nights of enthusiastically dreaming up projects, months would pass without his speaking again seriously even once about these subjects with the sultan. A year after the plague, when Grand Vizier Koprulu died, Hoja found another pretext for optimism: the sultan had hesitated to put his plans into practice because he'd feared Koprulu's power and personality, and now that the grand vizier had died and his son, less powerful than the father, had taken his place, it was time to expect courageous decisions from the sultan.

But we spent the next three years waiting for them. What bewildered me now was not the inactivity of the sultan, who was dazzled by his dreams and his hunting excursions, but that Hoja could still fix his hopes on him. All these years I'd been waiting for the day when he would lose hope and become like me! Although he no longer talked as much as he used to about 'victory', and didn't feel that exhilaration he had during the months following the plague, he was still able to keep alive his dream of a day when he would be able to manipulate the sultan with what he called his 'grand plan'. He could always find an excuse: right after that great fire that reduced Istanbul to rubble, the sultan's lavish investments in grand plans gave his enemies their opportunity of conspiring to put his brother on the throne; the sultan's hands were tied for the time being because the army had left on an expedition to the land of the Huns; the following year we expected them to begin an offensive against the Germans; then there was still the completion of the New Valide Mosque on the shores of the Golden Horn where Hoja often went with the sovereign and his mother Turhan Sultana, and for which great sums were being spent; there were also those endless hunting excursions in which I didn't take part. While I waited at home for Hoja to return from the hunt, I'd try to follow his instructions and come up with bright ideas for that 'grand plan' or 'science', dozing lazily as I turned the pages of his books.

It no longer amused me even to daydream about these projects; I cared little about the results they would yield should they ever be realized. Hoja knew as well as I did that there was nothing of substance in our thoughts about astronomy, geography, or even natural science during the years we first knew each other; the clocks, instruments, and models had been forgotten in a corner and long since gone to rust. We had postponed everything till the day when we would practise this obscure business he called 'science'; we had in hand not a grand plan that would save us from ruin, but only the dream of such a plan. In order to believe in this drab illusion, which didn't deceive me at all, and to feel a sense of camaraderie with Hoja, I tried sometimes to look with his eyes at the pages I turned, or put myself in his place as thoughts occurred to me at random. When he'd return from the hunt, I'd act as if I had discovered a new truth about whatever subject he'd left me to wear out my mind on, and that we could change everything in its light: when I said: 'The cause of the rising and falling of the sea is related to the heat of the rivers emptying into it', or, 'The plague is spread by tiny dust-motes in the air, and when the weather changes, it goes away', or, 'The Earth revolves around the sun, and the sun around the moon', Hoja, changing out of his dusty hunting costume, always gave me the same answer, making me smile with love: 'And the idiots here don't even realize this!'

Then he'd explode in a fit of rage which dragged me along in its fury, rave for hours about how the sovereign had chased after a stunned boar, or what nonsense it was for him to shed tears over a rabbit he'd had the greyhounds catch, admit against his will that what he'd said to the sultan during the hunt went in one ear and out the other, and ask rancorously over and over again when these idiots were going to realize the truth. Was it mere coincidence that so many fools were collected together in one place or was it inevitable? Why were they so stupid?

Thus he gradually came to feel he must begin anew with the thing he called 'science', this time in order to understand the nature of their minds. Since it reminded me of those days I loved when we had sat at the same table and, despising each other, been so alike, I was as enthusiastic as Hoja to start again on our 'science', but after some initial attempts we understood that things were not as they had been.

First of all, since I didn't know how to lead him on or why I should, I just couldn't pressure him. More important, I felt as if his sufferings and defeats were my own. On one occasion I reminded him of the folly of the people here, giving exaggerated examples, and made him feel he was as doomed to failure as they were – although I didn't believe this – and then observed his reaction. Although he disagreed with me violently, saying failure was not an inevitability if we acted first and devoted ourselves to this task – if, for example, we could realize the project of that weapon, we could still turn the tide of this river of history that was pushing us backwards – and although he made me happy by speaking not of his plans but of 'our' plans, as he did when he despaired, nevertheless he dreaded the approach of an inescapable defeat. I thought of him as an orphaned child, I loved his rage and sadness that reminded me of my first years of slavery; and I wanted to be like him. While he paced up and down the room looking out at the filthy, muddy streets under a dark rain or the washed-out, trembling lamps still burning from a couple of houses on the shores of the Golden Horn, as if he were searching there for some indication of a new sign he could pin his hopes on, it seemed for a moment that what paced, agonized, inside this room was not Hoja, but my own youth. The person I once had been had left me and was gone, and the I that was now dozing in a corner jealously desired him, as if in him I could recover the enthusiasm I had lost.

But I had also finally grown weary of this enthusiasm

that never tired of regenerating itself. After Hoja became imperial astrologer his property at Gebze had increased and our income had grown. There was no need for him to do anything more than chat with the sultan now and then. Once in a while we'd go to Gebze, tour the dilapidated mills and villages where wild sheepdogs were the first to greet us, check on the income, rummage through the accounts and try to figure out how much the overseer had cheated us. We'd write entertaining treatises for the sovereign, sometimes laughing but most of the time groaning with boredom, and that was all we did. If I hadn't insisted, he probably would not have arranged for those interludes when we'd lie with luxuriously perfumed prostitutes after idling away our days.

What unnerved him more was that the sovereign, encouraged by the absence of the army and the pashas who abandoned the city for the German campaign or the Cretan fortress, and because his mother couldn't force him to listen to her, had gathered around him again all those chattering wiseacres, buffoons, and impersonators who'd been driven from the palace. So as to set himself apart from these fakes whom he viewed with hatred and disgust and make them accept his superiority, Hoja was determined not to mingle with them, but when the sovereign insisted then he had no recourse but to talk with them and listen to their debates. After these gatherings discussing such questions as whether or not animals had souls, if so which ones, and which would go to heaven and which to hell, whether mussels were male or female, whether the sun that rises each morning is a new sun or simply the same sun that sets in the morning on the other side, he'd emerge despairing of the future, saying that if we did not take action the sultan would soon be beyond his grasp.

Because he talked about 'our' plans, 'our' future, I happily went along with him. Once, to try to grasp what was on the sultan's mind, we went through the notebooks I'd kept for years, our dreams, our memories. As if we were enumerating the contents of the drawers of a chest, we tried to tally the contents of the sovereign's mind; the result was not at all encouraging: although Hoja was still able to chatter enthusiastically about the incredible weapon that would be our salvation, or about the mysteries to be solved still hidden in the recesses of our minds, now he could no longer behave as if he didn't anticipate some catastrophic defeat drawing near. For months we wore ourselves out discussing this subject.

Did we understand 'defeat' to mean that the empire would lose all of its territories one by one? We'd lay out our maps on the table and mournfully determine first which territories, then which mountains or rivers would be lost. Or did defeat mean that people would change and alter their beliefs without noticing it? We imagined how everyone in Istanbul might rise from their warm beds one morning as changed people; they wouldn't know how to wear their clothes, wouldn't be able to remember what minarets were for. Or perhaps defeat meant to accept the superiority of others and try to emulate them: then he would recount some episode from my life in Venice, and we would imagine how acquaintances of ours here would act out my experiences dressed up with foreign hats on their heads and pants on their legs.

As a last resort we decided to present the sultan with these dreams that made us forget how we passed the time as we invented them. We thought that perhaps all these visions of defeat, brought to life in the vivid shades of our fantasies, might spur him to action. So, during the silent, dark nights, we filled a book with all the visions that flowed from the fantasies of defeat and failure we had dreamed up with a sad, despairing joy: those paupers with heads bowed, muddy roads, buildings left half-finished, dark, strange streets, people pleading that everything might be as it once was while they recited prayers they didn't understand, grieving mothers and fathers, unhappy men whose lives were too short for them to pass on to us what had been accomplished and recorded in other lands, machines left idle, souls whose eyes were moist from lamenting for the good old days, stray dogs reduced to skin and bones, villagers without any land, vagabonds wandering wildly through the city, illiterate Muslims wearing pants and all the wars ending in defeat. We put my faded memories in another part of the book: a few scenes from the happy and instructive experiences of my schooldays in Venice with my mother, father, and brothers and sisters: those who would conquer us live like this, and we must take action before they do and emulate them! In the conclusion our left-handed calligrapher copied out there was a well-measured verse which, using the metaphor of the cluttered cupboard Hoja loved so well, could be considered a door opening into the black puzzle of our minds' intricate mysteries. The finely woven mist of this poetry, majestic and silent in its own way, caught the sad essence of all the books and treatises I had written with Hoja.

Only a month after Hoja had submitted this book, the sultan ordered us to start work on that incredible weapon. We were bewildered by his command, and could never decide how far our success was due to this book.

9

When the sultan said, 'Let us see this incredible weapon that will ruin our enemies', perhaps he was testing Hoja, perhaps he'd had a dream he'd kept from Hoja, perhaps he wanted to show his domineering mother and the pashas who harassed him that the 'philosophers' he kept around were good for something, perhaps he thought Hoja might work another miracle after the plague, perhaps he'd truly been affected by those images of defeat we'd filled our book with, or perhaps it was the few actual military failures he'd suffered rather than our images of defeat which had alarmed him with the thought that, as he'd feared, those who wanted to put his brother in his place would drive him from the throne. We considered all these possibilities as we calculated in a daze the tremendous income that would come from the villages, caravansarays, and olive-groves the sovereign had granted us to finance the weapon.

Hoja decided that we should be surprised only by our own surprise: were they false, all those stories he'd told the sultan year after year, the treatises and books we'd written, that we should now have doubts when he believed them? And there was more: the sovereign had begun to be curious about what went on in the darkness of our minds. Hoja excitedly asked me if this wasn't the victory we'd waited for so long.

It was, and this time we had begun work as partners; since I was less anxious than he was about the result, I too was happy. During the next six years, while he worked to develop the weapon, we were in constant danger. Not because we worked with gunpowder, but because we drew upon ourselves the envy of our enemies; because everyone waited impatiently for us to triumph or fail; and we were in danger because we, too, waited in fear for the same things.

First we wasted a winter just working at the table. We were excited, enthusiastic, but had nothing more to hand than the idea of the weapon and the obscure and formless notions that haunted us when we imagined how it would crush our enemies. Later we decided to go out in the open air and experiment with gunpowder. Just as in the weeks of preparing the fireworks display, our men mixed the compounds in proportions we prescribed, then touched them off from a safe distance while we withdrew into the cool shadows under the tall trees. Curiosity-seekers came from the four corners of Istanbul to watch the colourful smoke exploding with various levels of noise. With time the crowds made a fairground of the field where we set up our tents, our targets and the short and long-barrelled cannon we had cast. One day at the end of summer, the sultan himself appeared without warning.

We put on a display for him, rocking earth and sky with sound; one by one we displayed the cartridge cases and shells we'd had prepared with well-primed gunpowder mixtures, the plans for the moulds of new guns and long-barrelled cannon not yet cast, the timed firing mechanisms that seemed to detonate by themselves. He showed more interest in me than he did in them. Hoja had wanted to keep me away from the sultan at first but when the display began and the sovereign saw that I gave the orders as often as Hoja, that our men looked to me as much as to him, he became curious.

As I was ushered into his presence for the second time after fifteen years, the sultan looked at me as if I were someone he'd met before but could not immediately place. He was like someone trying to identify a fruit he was tasting with his eyes shut. I kissed the hem of his skirt. He was not disturbed when he learned that I'd been here for twenty years but still had not become a Muslim. He had something else on his mind: 'Twenty years?' he said, 'How strange!' Then he suddenly asked me that question: 'Is it you who are teaching him all this?' He apparently hadn't asked this in order to learn my answer, for he left our tattered tent which smelled of gunpowder and saltpetre, and was walking towards his beautiful white horse when suddenly he stopped, turned towards the two of us just then standing side by side, and smiled all at once as if he'd seen one of those matchless wonders God created to break the pride of mankind, to make them sense their absurdity – a perfect dwarf or twin brothers alike as peas in a pod.

That night I was thinking about the sultan, but not in the way Hoja wanted me to. He continued to speak of him with disgust, but I had realized I would not be able to feel hatred or contempt: I was charmed by his informality, his sweetness, that air of a spoiled child who said whatever came to his mind. I wanted to be like him or to be his friend. After Hoja's angry outburst I lay in my bed trying to sleep, reflecting that the sultan did not seem to be someone who deserved to be duped; I wanted to tell him everything. But what exactly was everything?

My interest didn't go unreciprocated. One day when Hoja grudgingly said that the sovereign expected me too that morning, I went with him. It was one of those autumn days that smell of the sea. We spent the whole morning by a lily-pond under the plane-trees in a great forest covered with fallen red leaves. The sultan wanted to talk about the wriggling frogs that filled the pond. Hoja wouldn't indulge him, and only repeated a few clichés devoid of imagery and colour. The sultan didn't even notice the rudeness that shocked me so much. He was more interested in me.

So I spoke at length about the mechanics of how frogs jumped, about their circulatory systems, how their hearts continued to beat for a long time if carefully removed from their bodies, about the flies and insects they ate. I asked for pen and paper to demonstrate more clearly the stages an egg underwent to become a mature frog in the pond. The sovereign watched attentively while I drew pictures with the set of reed pens brought in a silver case inlaid with rubies. He listened with obvious pleasure to the stories I remembered about frogs and when I came to the part about the princess kissing the frog he gagged and made a sour face, but still did not resemble the foolish adolescent Hoja had described; he was more like a serious-minded adult who insisted on starting each day with science and art. At the end of those serene hours that Hoja frowned his way through, the sultan looked at the pictures of frogs in his hand and said 'I had always suspected it was you who made up his stories. So you drew the pictures as well!' Then he asked me about mustachioed frogs.

This was how my relationship with the sultan began. Now I accompanied Hoja every time he went to the palace. In the beginning Hoja said little, I did most of the talking to the sultan. While I spoke with him about his dreams, his enthusiasms, his fears, about the past and future, I'd wonder to what degree this good-humoured, intelligent man in front of me resembled the sultan Hoja had talked about year after year. I could tell from the clever questions he asked, from his shrewdness, that ever since he'd received the books we presented to him the sultan had been speculating how much of Hoja was me, and how much of me was Hoja. As for Hoja, at that time he was too busy with the cannon and the long barrels he was trying to get cast to be interested in these speculations, which he found idiotic anyway.

Six months after we began work on the cannon Hoja was alarmed to learn that the imperial master-general of artillery was furious that we were poking our noses into these affairs, and the man demanded either to be removed from office himself or to have crazy fools like us, who brought the craft of gunnery into disrepute with our belief that we were inventing something new, run out of Istanbul. But Hoja didn't look for a compromise, even though the imperial master-general did seem willing to reach an agreement. A month later, when the sultan ordered us to develop the weapon in a way that would not involve cannon, Hoja was not terribly disturbed. We both knew now that the new guns and long-barrelled cannon we'd had cast were no better than the old sort that had been used for years.

So according to Hoja we had entered yet another new phase in which we would dream up everything anew from the beginning, but because I'd now grown used to his rages and his dreams, the only thing that was new for me was getting to know the sovereign. And the sultan enjoyed our company. Like an attentive father who separates two brothers arguing over their marbles, saying "this one is yours, and this one is yours', he disentangled us with his observations about our speech and behaviour. These observations, which I found sometimes childish and sometimes clever, started to worry me: I began to believe that my personality had split itself off from me and united with Hoja's, and vice versa, without our perceiving it, and that the sultan, by evaluating this imaginary creature, had come to know us better than we knew ourselves.

While we interpreted his dreams, or talked about the new weapon – and in those days we had only our own dreams of it to struggle with – the sovereign would stop suddenly and, turning to one of us, say, 'No, this is his thought, not yours.' And sometimes he'd distinguish between our actions: 'Now you are glancing around just as he does. Be yourself!' When I laughed in surprise he'd continue, 'That's better, bravo. Have you two never looked at yourselves in the mirror together?' He'd ask which of us could stand to be himself when we did look in the mirror. On one occasion he'd ordered that all those treatises, bestiaries, and calendars we'd written for him over the years be brought out, and said that when he'd first read them, he'd tried to imagine as he turned the pages one by one which of us had written which parts, and even which parts one of us had written by putting himself in the other's place. But it was that

115

impersonator he had summoned while we attended him who really made Hoja angry, and enchanted me while utterly bewildering me as well.

This man resembled us neither in face nor form, he was short and fat, and his dress completely different, but when he began to speak I was shocked; it was as if Hoja, not he, were talking. Like Hoja, he'd lean towards the sovereign's ear as if whispering a secret, like Hoja he made his voice grow grave with a studied, thoughtful air when he discussed finer points, and suddenly, just like Hoja, he'd be swept up in the excitement of what he was saying, passionately wave his hands and arms in order to persuade his interlocutor and be left breathless; but although he spoke with Hoja's accent he didn't describe projects related to the stars or incredible weapons, he merely enumerated the dishes he'd learned in the palace kitchen and the ingredients and spices necessary to prepare them. While the sultan smiled, the mimic continued with his impersonation, which turned Hoja's face upside-down, by listing the caravansarays between Istanbul and Aleppo one by one. Then the sultan asked the mimic to imitate me. That man who looked at me with his mouth hanging open in shock was me: I was stupefied. When the sovereign asked him to impersonate someone who was half Hoja and half me, I was totally bewitched. Watching the man's movements I felt like saying, just as the sultan had, 'This is me, and this is Hoja', but the mimic did this himself by pointing with his finger at each of us in turn. After the sultan praised the man and sent him away, he ordered us to reflect on what we'd seen.

What did he mean? That evening when I told Hoja that the sultan was a much cleverer man than the person he'd been describing to me for years, and said the sultan had found for himself the direction Hoja wanted to lead him in, Hoja flew into a rage once more. This time I felt he had cause: the mimic's art was not to be endured. Hoja said he would not set foot in the palace again unless he was forced to. He had no intention, now the opportunity he'd waited for all these years had at last come within his grasp, of humiliating himself by wasting time with those fools. Since I knew the sultan's enthusiasms and had the wit to play the buffoon, I would go to the palace in his place.

When I told the sovereign that Hoja was ill, he didn't believe me. 'Let him work on the weapon,' he said. Thus during those four years while Hoja planned and brought the weapon to completion, I went to the palace and he stayed at home with his dreams as I used to do.

In these four years I learned that life was to be enjoyed rather than merely endured. Those who saw that the sovereign esteemed me as he did Hoja soon invited me to the ceremonies and celebrations which were the daily palace fare. One day a vizier's daughter was getting married, the next day one more child was born to the sovereign, his sons' circumcisions were marked by festival, another day they celebrated the recapture of a castle from the Hungarians, then ceremonies were arranged to mark the prince's first day at school, while Ramadan and other holiday festivities began. I quickly grew fat from stuffing myself with rich meats and pilaus and gobbling down sugar lions, ostriches, mermaids and nuts at these festivities, most of which lasted for days. The greater part of my time was spent watching spectacles: wrestlers, their skin glistening with oil, struggling till they fainted, or tightrope-walkers on high-wires stretched between the minarets of mosques who juggled with the clubs they carried on their backs, crushed horseshoe nails with their teeth, and stabbed themselves with knives and skewers, or conjurors who produced snakes, doves, and monkeys from their robes, making the coffee cups in our hands and the money in our pockets disappear in the twinkling of an eye, or the shadow-plays of Karagoz and Hajivat whose obscenities I adored. At night, if there were no fireworks display, I'd follow my new friends, most of whom I'd met that same day, to one of those palaces or mansions where everyone went and after drinking raki or wine and listening to music for hours, I'd enjoy myself clinking glasses with beautiful girl dancers who imitated languorous gazelles, handsome boys who walked on water, vocalists with their burning voices who sang sensitive and joyous songs.

I'd often go to the mansions of the ambassadors who were so curious about me, and after watching a ballet of girls and boys stretching their lovely limbs, or listening to the latest pretentious nonsense played by an orchestra brought from Venice, I would enjoy the benefits of my gradually increasing fame. The Europeans gathered at the embassies would ask me about the terrifying adventures I'd lived through, they wondered how much I'd suffered, how I'd endured, how I was still able to go on. I'd conceal the fact that I had passed my whole life dozing within four walls writing silly books, and tell them incredible stories which I'd learned to extemporize, just as I did with the sultan, about this exotic land which so fascinated them. Not only the young women making their pre-nuptial appearances before their fathers, and the ambassadors' wives who flirted with me, but all those dignified ambassadors and officials listened full of admiration to the bloody tales of religion and violence, intrigues of love and the harem, that I invented. If they pressed me, I'd whisper one or two state secrets or describe some strange habits of the sultan no one could know of which I'd make up on the spot. When they wanted more information, I'd enjoy giving myself a secretive air; I'd act as if I couldn't say everything I knew, I'd take refuge in a silence which inflamed the curiosity of these fools Hoja wanted us to emulate. But I knew they whispered amongst themselves that I was involved in some grand and mysterious project requiring mastery of science, some design for an obscure weapon requiring a stupendous amount of money.

When I returned in the evenings from these mansions, these palaces, my mind filled with the images of the beautiful bodies I'd seen, and fogged by the vapours of the spirits I'd drunk, I would find Hoja sitting at our twenty-year-old table. He'd thrown himself into his work with an urgency I had never seen in him before, the table loaded with strange models I couldn't make sense of, drawings, pages covered with desperate scribblings. He'd ask me to recount what I'd seen and done all day, but he was soon disgusted by these pastimes which he found shameless and stupid, so he'd interrupt me and begin to describe his plan, speaking of 'us' and 'them'.

He'd repeat once again that everything was connected with the unknown inner landscape of our minds, he'd based his whole project on this, he talked excitedly about the symmetry, or the chaos, of the cupboard full of junk we call the brain, but I could not understand how this might serve as a point of departure for designing the weapon on which he'd set all his hopes, all our hopes. I doubted that anyone – including him, contrary to what I'd once thought – would be capable of fathoming this. He declared that one day someone would open up our heads and prove all these ideas of his. He spoke of a great truth he'd perceived during the days of the plague when we had contemplated ourselves in the mirror together: now all of it had achieved clarity in his mind, you see, the weapon had its genesis in this moment of truth! Then he would point out to me – moved as I was, without understanding – a bizarre, obscure, ambiguous shape on paper with the tips of his trembling fingers.

This shape, which I saw slightly more developed each time he showed it to me, seemed to remind me of something. While I looked at that black stain I will call the 'devil' of the drawing, I would be on the point of suddenly saying what it reminded me of, but suffering a moment's hesitation, or thinking my mind was playing tricks on me, I'd keep silent. All during those four years I never clearly perceived this shape he scattered over pages, giving it a sharper definition as it developed a little more each time, and which, after consuming all that effort and money accumulated over the years, he was at last able to bring to life. Sometimes I likened it to things in our daily life, sometimes to images in our dreams, once or twice to things we saw or talked about in the old days when we recounted our memories to one another, but I was unable to take the final step of clarifying the images that passed through my mind, so I'd submit to the confusion of my thoughts, and waited in vain for the weapon itself to reveal its mystery. Even four years later, when that little stain had been transformed into a bizarre creature as tall as a grand mosque, a terrifying apparition which all Istanbul talked about and Hoja called a real machine of war, and while everyone likened it to one thing or another, I was still lost in the details of what Hoja had told me in the past about how the weapon would triumph in the future.

Like someone waking up and struggling to remember a dream that memory stubbornly wants to forget, on my visits to the palace I would try to repeat these vivid, terrifying details for the sultan. I would speak of those wheels, the catapult, the dome, the gunpowder and levers that Hoja had described to me who knows how many times. The words were not my words, and although there was none of the fire of Hoja's passion in what I said, still I saw that the sovereign was affected. And it moved me too that this man, whom I found serious-minded, was inspired with hope by this obscure mass of speech, my crude rendition of Hoja's fervent poetry of victory and salvation. The sovereign would say that Hoja, the man sitting at home, was me. These intellectual games of his thoroughly confused my mind but no longer took me by surprise. When he said that I was Hoja, I'd think it better not to follow his logic, for soon he'd assert that I was the one who had taught Hoja all of these things – not the lethargic person I was now, but the one who had changed Hoja long ago. If only we would talk about the entertainments, the animals, the festivals of the old days, or the preparations for the shopkeepers' parade, I thought. Later the sultan said everyone knew that I was behind this project of the weapon.

This was what frightened me most. Hoja had not been

seen in public for years, he was almost forgotten, I was the one appearing so often at the sovereign's side in the palaces, in the city, and now they were jealous of me! They were grinding their teeth at me, the infidel, not just because the income from so many herds of sheep, olive-groves, cara-vansarays, was tied up in this obscure plan for a weapon they gossipped about more and more each day, not just because I was so close to the sultan, but also because by working on this weapon we were poking our noses in other people's business. When I couldn't shut my ears against their slander, I would reveal my fears to Hoja or the sultan.

But they were not very responsive. Hoja had buried him-self completely in his work. I longed for his anger as old men long for the passion of youth. During those last months while he nourished that dark and ambiguous stain on paper with details and transformed it into designs for the mould of a freakish monster, pouring out incredible amounts of money for the moulds and casting with iron too heavy for any cannon to penetrate, he didn't even listen to the evil gossip I related to him; he showed interest only in the ambassadors' mansions where they were talking about his work: what kind of men were these ambassadors, what did they think, did they have any opinion about this weapon? And most important: why did the sultan never think of sending envoys to establish embassies representing the Empire in those countries? I sensed he wanted this post for himself, wanted to escape from the idiots here and live among them, but he never spoke openly of this desire, even on the days when he despaired of ever realizing his design, when the iron he'd cast had cracked, or he believed he would run out of money. He let slip only once or twice that he wanted to establish relations with 'their' men of science; perhaps they would understand the truths he'd discovered about the insides of our heads; he wanted to correspond with men of science in Venice, Flanders, whatever faraway land occurred to him at the moment. Who were the very best among them, where did they live, how could one

121

correspond with them, could I learn these things from the ambassadors? In those last days I took little interest in the weapon finally being realized and gave myself over to pleasure, forgetting these hopes of his, with their traces of a despondency our rivals would have found amusing.

The sultan too had turned a deaf ear to our enemies' gossip. During the days when Hoja, ready to test the weapon, was looking for brave men to enter that terrifying mountain of metal and turn the flywheels while choking in the stench of rusting iron, the sultan didn't even listen as I complained about the rumours. As he always did, he made me repeat what Hoja had been saying. He believed in him, was content with everything, didn't at all regret having put his trust in him: for all of this he was grateful to me. Always for the same reason of course: because I had taught Hoja everything. Like Hoja, he too talked about the insides of our heads; and then he'd bring up the other question akin to this interest of his; just as Hoja had done once upon a time, the sultan would ask me how they lived in that land, in my old country.

I regaled him with dreams. I can't tell now whether these stories, most of which I have come to believe myself after repeating them so often, were things I actually experienced in my youth or visions which flowed from my pen every time I sat down at the table to write my book; sometimes I'd throw in a couple of amusing falsehoods which sprang to mind. I had certain fables which had grown with re-telling, since the sovereign showed interest in the detail that the clothes people wore had lots of buttons, I'd make sure to repeat this and told stories that I wasn't sure were from memories or my dreams. But there were also things I had still not been able to forget after twenty-five years, things that were real: the talks I had with my mother and father, my brothers and sisters while breakfasting at the family table under the linden-trees! These were the details which least interested the sultan. He had said to me once that basically every life was like another. This frightened me for

122

some reason: there was a devilish expression on the sultan's face I'd never seen before, and I wanted to ask what he meant by this. While I looked apprehensively into his face, I felt an impulse to say 'I am I'. It was as if, had I been able to find the courage to speak this nonsensical phrase, I would obliterate all those games played by all those gossips scheming to turn me into someone else, played by Hoja and the sultan, and live at peace again within my own being. But like those who shy away from even the mention of any uncertainty that might jeopardize their security, I kept silent in fear.

This happened in the spring, in the days when Hoja had finished work on the weapon but had not yet been able to test it because he couldn't assemble the team of men he needed. Soon after, we were shocked when the sovereign left with the army on an expedition to the land of the Poles. Why had he not taken the ultimate weapon along with him, why hadn't he taken me, didn't he trust us? Like the rest of those left behind in Istanbul, we believed the sultan had gone not to war but to hunt. Hoja was happy to have gained one more year; since I had no other occupation or entertainment, we worked on the weapon together.

It was a great struggle recruiting men to operate the machine. No one was willing to go inside the terrifying, mysterious vehicle. Hoja let it be known he would pay very well, we sent criers out into the city, to the shipyards, the cannon foundries, searched for men among the idlers in the coffee-houses, the homeless, the adventurous. Most of the men we were able to find, even if they overcame their fear and went inside the iron heap, soon ran away, unable to endure operating the flywheels while crammed into that bizarre insect cooking in the heat. When we were able to get the vehicle moving at the end of summer, all the money accumulated over the years for the project had run out. The weapon stirred clumsily under the bewildered and frightened gaze of the curious, and to shouts of victory it weaved from right to left attacking an imaginary fortress, fired its shells, then stopped still. Money continued to pour in from our villages and olive-groves, but the team we had gathered proved too expensive to maintain and Hoja was forced to let the men go.

Winter passed in waiting. The sovereign had stopped in his beloved Edirne on his return from the expedition; no one sought us out, we were left to ourselves. Since there was no one in the morning at the palace for us to entertain with our stories, and no one for me to be entertained by in the mansions in the evenings, we had nothing to do. I tried to while away the days having my portrait done by a painter from Venice and taking music lessons on the oud; Hoja went every other minute to Kuledibi by the old walls to look at his weapon which he had left a watchman to guard. He could not resist adding a few things to it here and there, but soon tired of this. During the nights of the last winter we spent together, he mentioned neither the weapon nor his plans for it. A lethargy had descended on him, but not because he had lost his passion – he was like this because I no longer inspired him.

At night we'd spend most of our time waiting, waiting for the wind or the snow to stop, waiting for the last cries of the peddlers passing by in the street late at night, for the fire to die down so we could put more wood in the stove. On one of those winter nights during which we spoke very little, often drifting off into our own thoughts, Hoja suddenly said I had much changed, that I had finally become a completely different person. My stomach burned, I began to sweat; I wanted to make a stand against him, to tell him he was wrong, tell him that I was as I had always been, that we were alike, that he should pay attention to me the way he used to do, that we still had many, many things to talk about, but he was right; my eye was caught by the portrait of myself I had brought home that morning and left leaning against a wall. I had changed: I'd grown fat from stuffing myself at feasts, I had a double chin, my flesh had become slack, my movements slow; worse, my face was completely different; a coarse expression had crept into the corners of my mouth from drinking and making love at those bacchanals, my eyes were languid from sleeping at odd times, from passing out drunk, and like those fools who are content with their lives, the world, themselves, there was a crude smugness in my glance, but I knew I was content with my new state: I said nothing.

Later, up until the time we learned the sultan had summoned us and our weapon to Edirne for the campaign, I had a recurring dream: we were at a masked ball in Venice reminiscent in its confusion of the feasts of Istanbul: when the 'courtesans' took off their masks I recognized my mother and fiancée in the crowd, and I took off my own mask full of hope that they would recognize me too, but somehow they didn't know it was me, they were pointing with their masks to someone behind me; when I turned to look, I saw that this person who would know that I was me was Hoja. Then when I approached him, in the hope that he would recognize me, the man who was Hoja took off his mask without a word and from behind it, terrifying me with a pang of guilt that woke me from my dream, emerged the image of my youth.

10

Hoja finally sprang into action at the beginning of summer, the moment he learned the sultan expected us and the weapon at Edirne. It was then I realized he'd kept everything ready, maintaining contact all winter long with the group of men who had operated the weapon. In three days we were ready for the campaign. Hoja passed the night of the last day as if we were moving to a new house, rummaging through his old books with torn bindings, half-finished treatises, yellowing first drafts, his personal things and so forth. He got his rusty prayer-clock working, dusted off his astronomical instruments. He was up till dawn examining twenty-five years' worth of rough drafts of books, models and sketches of weapons. At sunrise I saw him turning the torn, yellowed pages of the little notebook I'd filled with observations from our experiments for that first fireworks display. He asked shyly: should we take these with us?; would they be of use did I think? When he saw me look at him blankly, he threw the things into a corner in disgust.

Nevertheless, on this ten-day trip to Edirne we felt close to one another, even if less than in the old days. Above all, Hoja was optimistic; our weapon that they called freak, insect, satan, turtle archer, walking tower, iron heap, red rooster, kettle on wheels, giant, cyclops, monster, swine, gypsy, blue-eyed weirdie, took to the road very slowly with a bizarre uproar of frightening screeches and groans, striking all who saw it with exactly the terror that Hoja intended, and was moving forward more speedily than he'd expected. It delighted him to see the curious gather from the surrounding villages and line up on the hills along the road, straining to get a view of the machine they feared to approach. At night, in the silence measured by crickets, when our men had fallen into a deep sleep in their tents after sweating blood and tears all day long, Hoja would describe to me the devastation his red rooster was going to wreak upon our enemies. True, he was not as exuberant as he had been, and like me he worried about the reaction the sovereign's circle and the army would have to the weapon, what kind of position it would be given in the attack formation, but he was still able to speak with satisfaction and certainty of our 'last chance', of how we had been able to turn the tide in our favour, and more importantly, of the 'them and us' for whom he never lost his mania.

The weapon entered Edirne with a ceremony only the sovereign and a few shameless sycophants in his retinue welcomed with any warmth. The sultan received Hoja like an old friend, there were rumours of the possibility of war, but little preparation or haste; they began to spend their days together. I joined them as well; when they mounted their horses and rode to the surrounding dark woods to listen to the birds singing, or took excursions by boat down the Tunja and Merich Rivers to watch the frogs, or went to pet the storks that had been clawed in fights with eagles and wailed in the courtyard of the Selimiye Mosque, or to watch the weapon execute its manoeuvres once more, I was always with them. But I realized with chagrin that I had nothing to contribute to their conversations, nothing I could say to them sincerely or that they would find interesting. Perhaps I was jealous of their intimacy. But I knew I was finally sick of it all. Hoja was still reciting the same poetry and by then it shocked me to see how the sovereign was taken in by the same trumped-up tale of victory, of 'their' superiority, of how the time had come for us to rouse ourselves at last and take action, of the future and the mysteries of our minds.

One day, midway through a summer thick with rumours of war, Hoja said he had need of a strong companion and asked me to come with him. We walked quickly through Edirne, passing through the gypsy and Jewish neighbourhoods down some ashen streets I had wandered through before with the sense of oppression that came over me now again, passing the houses of poor Muslims most of which were indistinguishable from one another. Eventually when I realized the ivy-covered houses I had seen on my left were now on my right, I understood we had retraced our steps; I enquired, and was told we were in the district of Fildami. Hoja suddenly knocked at the door of one house. A green-eyed child about eight years old opened the door. 'Lions,' said Hoja to him, 'lions have escaped from the sultan's palace, we're making a search.' He shoved the child aside and entered the house with me at his heels. We hurried through the half-darkness of the interior smelling of sawdust and soap, up some creaking stairs into a long hall on the upper floor; Hoja began to open the doors leading off it. In the first room there was an old man dozing, his toothless mouth wide open, and two laughing children reaching for his beard who jumped when they saw the door opening. Hoja closed that door and opened another; there was a pile of quilts and quilting material inside. The child who had opened the street door grabbed the handle of the door to the third room before Hoja did, saying, 'There are no lions here, just my mother and auntie,' but Hoja opened the door anyway on two women with their backs turned towards us performing their prayers in the pale light. In the fourth room a man stitching a quilt, who resembled me more because he was unbearded, rose when he saw Hoja. 'You madman, what are you doing here?' he cried. 'What do you want from us?' 'Where is Semra?' said Hoja. 'She went to Istanbul ten years ago,' the man said. 'We heard she died of plague. Why haven't you croaked as well?' Without saying a word Hoja went down the stairs and left the house. As I followed him I heard the child shouting behind me and

128

a woman answering him: 'The lions were here, Mother!' 'No child, your uncle and his brother!'

Perhaps because I could not bring myself to forget the past, or perhaps in preparation for my new life and this book you are still reading patiently, two weeks later I returned to that same place at dawn. At first, unable to see clearly in the early light, I had trouble finding the house; when I did, I tried to return by way of the road I guessed would be the quickest shortcut to the hospital of Beyazit Mosque. Perhaps because I was mistaken in thinking Hoja and his mother would have taken the quickest way, I couldn't find the short road shaded by poplar trees that led to the bridge; I did find a poplar-lined road, but there was no river near it where they might have rested eating halva so long ago. And at the hospital there were none of the things I'd imagined, it was not muddy but perfectly clean, there was no sound of running water, nor coloured bottles. When I saw a patient in chains I couldn't resist asking a doctor about him: he had fallen in love, gone mad, and believed he was someone else like most madmen; he would have told me more, but I left.

The decision to embark on the campaign we had thought would never come was made at the end of summer, on a day we least expected it: the Poles, who would not accept the defeat of the previous year and the heavy taxes which followed, sent the message: 'Come and collect the taxes with your swords.' While the attack formation was being planned, no one in the army gave any thought to the deployment of the weapon, and Hoja spent the next few days choking with rage; no one wanted to march into battle alongside this heap of wrought iron; no one expected anything useful from this gigantic kettle; worse, they believed it was an ill omen. On the day before the planned departure, while Hoja was examining the omens for the campaign, we heard that our rivals were stirring up talk and it was being said openly that the weapon could just as easily bring a curse as a victory. When Hoja told me people believed the responsibility for this curse lay with me rather than him, I was terrified. The sovereign announced his confidence in Hoja and the weapon, and to avoid any further dispute, commanded that during the battle the weapon would be directly attached to himself, to his own forces. At the beginning of September, on a hot day, we departed from Edirne.

Everyone thought it was late in the season for a campaign, but the matter was not discussed much: I was just beginning to learn that during a campaign the soldiers feared inauspicious omens as much as they did the enemy, sometimes more, that they were battling as much with this fear. On the first night, after marching north through prosperous villages over bridges that groaned under the weight of our weapon, we were surprised to be summoned to the sultan's tent. Like his soldiers the sovereign had suddenly become child-like, he had about him the air of a boy eager and excited at the start of a new game, and would ask Hoja, just as his soldiers did, for his interpretation of omens: the red cloud before the setting sun, the low-flying falcons, the broken chimney of a house in the village, the cranes pressing south, what did these things mean? Hoja of course interpreted them all favourably.

But apparently our work was not finished; we were both just finding out that on the journey the sovereign especially liked to be told strange, frightening stories at night-time. Hoja called up dark images from the passionate poetry of that book of ours I loved best, the one we had given the sultan years before – evil images swarming with corpses, bloody battles, defeats, treachery and misery – but he directed the sovereign's wide eyes to the flame of victory shining in a corner of this tableau: we must fan that flame with the bellows of our intelligence, 'theirs and ours', and realize the secret truths of the interior of our minds and all the other things Hoja had told me about for years which I now wanted to forget – we must rouse ourselves out of our somnolent state as soon as possible! I was becoming weary of these bitter tales, but each night Hoja increased a little more their gloom, the ugliness, the malevolence, perhaps because he thought even the sovereign was now becoming sated with the stories. Again I felt the sultan shiver with pleasure when Hoja mentioned the interior of our minds.

The hunting excursions began the week after our departure. A party that came along with the army solely for this purpose rode in advance, and after scouring the area, passing over the arable land and rousing the villagers, the sovereign, ourselves, and the hunters would gallop off from the march towards a forest that was famous for its gazelles, up the slopes of a mountain where wild boar ran, or into a wood teeming with foxes and hares. After these amusing little diversions, which lasted for hours, we'd return to the march with elaborate fanfare as if we were returning victoriously from battle, and while the army saluted the sovereign we would watch, standing directly behind him. Hoja endured these ceremonies with anger and hatred, but I loved them; I enjoyed talking with the sultan in the evenings about the hunt much more than about the march, the villages through which the army had passed or the condition of the towns and latest news of the enemy. Then Hoja, enraged at this chatter he found stupid and idiotic, would begin his stories and predictions that escalated in violence with every night that passed. Like others in his circle even I by now was pained to see the sovereign give credence to these tales that were meant to be frightening, these ghost stories about the dark recesses of the mind.

But I would be witness to even worse! We were hunting again; a nearby village had been evacuated, the locals were spread out through the forest, beating tin pots to drive boar and deer with all this clamour towards the spot where we waited with our horses and weapons. Yet by noon we had not seen even one animal. To relieve our weariness and the discomfort of the midday heat, the sovereign ordered Hoja to tell him some of those tales that made him shiver at night. We were moving along very slowly, listening to the barely perceptible roar of the tin pots coming from far away when, coming upon a Christian village, we halted. It was then I saw Hoja and the sultan point to one of the empty houses in the village and cajole a skinny old man stretching his head out of the door to come forward. A little earlier they had been talking about 'them' and the insides of their heads and now, when I saw the fascination on their faces and heard Hoja ask the old man a few things through the interpreter, I came closer, dreading the prospect. Hoja was questioning the old man, demanding he answer at once without thinking: what was his greatest transgression, the worst thing he had done in his life? The villager, in a Slav dialect the translator had difficulty interpreting for us, mumbled hoarsely that he was a blameless, innocent old man; but Hoja insisted with a peculiar vehemence that the old man should tell us about himself. Only when he saw that the sovereign was as attentive as Hoja did the old man confess that he had sinned: yes, he was guilty, he too should have left his house along with the rest of the village, he should have joined the hunt with his brothers and sisters as they chased the animals, but he was sick, he had an excuse, he was not healthy enough to run around in the forest all day, and when he gestured to his heart, asking forgiveness, Hoja became angry and shouted that he was asking about his real sins, not about that. The villager however could not understand the question our translator kept on repeating, he sorrowfully pressed his hand upon his heart, at a loss for anything else to say. They took the old man away. When the next one they brought said the same things, Hoja flushed bright red. He told this second villager about my childhood trangressions, the lies I'd told in order to be loved more than my brothers and sisters and the sexual indiscretions I'd committed while studying at the university, as if he were describing the crimes of an unnamed sinner, giving examples of wickedness and vice to prompt the villager, while I listened, remembering with revulsion and shame those days we spent together during the plague but which I recall now with longing as I write this book. When the

132

last villager they brought forward, a cripple, confessed in a whisper that he had secretly spied on women bathing in the river, Hoja calmed down a bit. Yes, you see, this was how they behaved when confronted with their sins, they were able to face up to them; but we, who supposedly understood by now what took place in the recesses of the mind, etc., etc. I wanted to believe the sultan was not impressed.

But his interest had been aroused; two days later he closed his eyes to a repetition of the same drama during another deer hunt, perhaps because he couldn't withstand Hoja's insistence, or perhaps because he had taken greater pleasure in the interrogations than I thought. By now we had crossed the Danube; again we were in a Christian village. As for the questions Hoja pressed on the villagers, there was little change in them. They reminded me of the violence of those nights during the plague when I succeeded in making him write down his sins, and at first I didn't even want to hear the replies of the villagers, who feared the questions and the man who asked them, this anonymous judge silently supported by the sultan. I was overcome by a strange nausea; more than Hoja I blamed the sovereign, who was either duped by him or unable to resist the attraction of this sinister game. But it was not long before I was gripped by the same fascination; a man loses nothing by listening, I thought, and drew near them. Most of the sins and misdeeds, told now in a delicate language more pleasing to my ear, resembled one another: simple lies, small deceptions; one or two dirty tricks, one or two infidelities; at most, a few petty thefts.

In the evening Hoja said that the villagers had not revealed everything, they were withholding the truth; I had gone much further in my writings: they must have committed sins much more profound, more real, that distinguished them from us. In order to convince the sultan, to get hold of these truths, to be able to prove what kind of men 'they', and furthermore 'we', were, he would use violence if necessary.

This distasteful brutality grew more virulent and sense-less with every passing day. In the beginning everything had been simpler; we had been like children playing, crack-ing a few coarse but harmless jokes between rounds in a game; each hour of interrogation was like a little skit between the acts of a play while we rested during our long and pleasurable hunting excursions; but as time went by they turned into rituals that sapped all our will, our patience, our nerve, but which we somehow could not forgo. I saw villagers stupefied with horror at Hoja's questions and his incomprehensible rage; if they could have understood exactly what was being asked of them, perhaps they would have complied: I saw toothless and tired old men herded into the village square; before they stuttered out their mis-deeds, real or imagined, they would beg for help from those around them, and from us, with hopeless eyes; I saw youths roughed up, knocked down and forced to stand again when their confessions and sins were not found satisfactory: I would remember how after reading what I'd written at the table Hoja had said, 'You rogue, you', and brought a fist down on my back, mumbling and worrying himself to death because he could not understand how I could be like that. But now he had a better idea of what he was looking for, what conclusion he wanted to reach, even if not pre-cisely. He tried other methods as well: half the time he'd interrupt the villager and insist that he was lying; then our men would rough up the offender. At other times he'd interrupt the man, claiming that one of his friends had con-tradicted him. For a while he tried calling them forward two by two. When he saw the confessions were superficial, and the villagers were ashamed before one another in spite of the violence that our men applied so purposefully, he'd fly into a rage.

By the time the relentless, heavy rains began I too was almost inured to what was happening. I remember the vil-lagers who said very little, and had little intention of saying very much, being beaten in vain and made to stand and wait soaking wet in the muddy square of a village hour after hour. As time went on the attractions of the hunt faded and our excursions were cut short. Occasionally we killed a sad-eyed gazelle or a fat wild boar, which grieved the sultan, but now we were preoccupied not with the details of the hunt but with these inquisitions for which the preparations, like those for a hunt, began well in advance. At night, as if he felt guilty for what he had done all day, Hoja poured out his feelings to me. He, too, was disturbed by what was happening, by the violence, but he wanted to prove something, something that would benefit all of us: he wanted to demonstrate it to the sultan as well; and besides, why were those villagers hiding the truth? Later he said we should perform the same experiment in a Muslim village for comparison; but this did not yield the results he'd wished: although he interrogated them with little coercion, the fact was that they made more or less the same confessions and told the same stories as their Christian neighbours. It was one of those miserable days when the rain would not let up, Hoja muttered a few words implying they were not true Muslims, but in the evening when the day's events were discussed I could see he realized this truth had not escaped the sultan's notice either.

This discovery only increased his anger and forced him to resort to even more violence than the sultan could bear to witness but which, perhaps like me, he followed with morbid curiosity. As we moved further and further north we came once again to a forested area where the villagers spoke a Slav dialect; in a quaint little village we saw Hoja beat with his own fists a handsome adolescent who could remember nothing more than a childish lie. Hoja swore he would never do this again; in the evening he was overcome by a sense of guilt that even I found excessive. On another occasion, while a yellowish rain was falling, I thought I saw the women of a village weeping from afar at what was being done to their men. Even our soldiers, who had become expert at their work, were sick of what was happening;

sometimes they would select the next man to confess before we did and bring him forward, and our translator asked the first questions himself instead of Hoja, who looked worn out by his rage. It was not that we never came across interesting victims who told of their sins at great length, as if deep down in their hearts they'd been waiting for years for this day of interrogation, terrified and bewildered either by tales of our violence, which we'd heard had travelled from village to village and become legend, or by the spectre of some absolute justice whose mystery they could not penetrate; but by now Hoja was no longer interested in the infidelities of husbands and wives, the stories of poor villagers who envied their rich neighbours. He continually repeated that there was a deeper truth, but I think he doubted now and then, as we did, whether we would be able to discover it. Or at least he sensed our doubt and flew into a rage, but we and the sultan all felt he had no intention of giving up. Perhaps for this reason we became resigned spectators, who watched him take the reins in his own hands. Once, sheltering from a sudden downpour under the edge of a roof, we grew hopeful at the sight of Hoja being soaked to the skin while he endlessly interrogated an adolescent who hated his stepfather and stepbrothers for mistreating his mother; but later in the evening, he closed the subject saying this one, too, was just a common adolescent not worth remembering.

We pressed north and further north; the march, twisting between the high mountains, inched forward very slowly on muddy roads through deep black forests. I loved the cool, dark air coming from the woods thick with pine and beech-trees, the misty silences awakening doubt, everything indistinct. Though no one called them by this name, I believe we were in the foothills of the Carpathian Mountains, which I'd seen in my childhood on a map of Europe my father had, one drawn by some mediocre artist who had decorated it with pictures of deer and Gothic châteaux. Hoja had caught cold in the rains and was ill, but we would still go into the forest every morning, breaking away from the march which was crawling along a road that twisted as if it wanted to delay ever reaching an end. We now seemed to have forgotten the hunting expeditions: it was as if we lingered at the shore of a lake or the edge of a precipice, not to shoot deer but rather to make the villagers who were preparing for us wait even longer! When we decided the time had come, we'd enter one of the villages, and after going through our ritual would trail along after Hoja who rushed us on to yet another village, never able to find the treasure he sought but desperate to forget those he manhandled and beat up, and his own despair. On one occasion he wanted to perform an experiment: the sultan, whose patience astounded me, had twenty janissaries brought forth for this purpose; he asked the same questions first of them, and then of the fair-haired villagers who stood dumbfounded in front of their houses. Another time he brought the villagers up to the march, showed them our weapon screeching and groaning while it strained to keep up with the sovereign's army on the muddy roads, asked them what they thought of it and had the scribes write down their answers, but his strength was exhausted. Perhaps it was because, as he claimed, we knew nothing of truth, or perhaps he too was intimidated by the meaningless violence, perhaps it was the feeling of guilt that came over him at night, or because he was sick of hearing the army and the pashas mutter disapprovingly about the weapon and the episodes in the forest, or perhaps simply because he was ill, I don't know: his hoarse voice did not boom out as it used to; he'd lost his old vigour in asking the questions whose answers he knew by heart; in the evenings when he spoke of victory, of the future, of how we must rise up and save ourselves, it was as if even his own voice, diminishing as time went by, did not believe what he was saying. The last image I have of him is interrogating a few bewildered Slav villagers without any conviction while a yellow rain the colour of sulphurous smoke was just starting up again. We didn't want to listen anymore and kept our distance; through the dreamy light flattened out by the rain, we saw them staring blankly at the wet surface of a huge mirror in a gilded frame that Hoja passed from hand to hand.

We did not go out on these 'hunting' expeditions again; we'd forded the river and entered the lands of the Poles. Our weapon could make no progress on roads which had turned to sodden clay in the filthy rain, growing heavier with every passing day, and it held back the march now we needed to move quickly. It was then that the rumours increased about how our siege engine – which the pashas already hated – would bring misfortune, even a curse upon us; these were spiced with the whisperings of the janissaries who had participated in Hoja's 'experiments'. As always it was not Hoja but me, the infidel, whom they blamed. When Hoja started up his patter, leavened with verse that now made even the sovereign impatient, and spoke of the indispensability of the weapon, of the enemy's strength, of how we must rouse ourselves and take action, the pashas listening to him in the sovereign's tent were even more firmly convinced that we were charlatans and our weapon would bring bad luck. They looked upon Hoja as a sick man who'd gone astray but was not beyond saving; the truly dangerous, truly guilty one, was I, who had deceived Hoja and the sovereign and concocted these ill-omened ideas. At night when we withdrew into our tents Hoja would revile the pashas in his ravaged voice the way he used to rail against his fools in years past, but there was nothing left of the joy and hope I believed we had been able to keep alive in those years.

I could see, however, that he was not about to give up yet. Two days later, when our weapon got stuck in the mud right in the middle of the line of march, I lost all hope; but Hoja continued to struggle, sick as he was. No one would spare us a man, not even a horse; he went to the sultan and found nearly forty horses, had them unhitched from the cannon, and collected a group of men; towards evening, after struggling all day under the gaze of those who prayed it would sink into the mud and stay there, he whipped the horses in a rage and made our monstrous insect move. He spent the evening arguing with the pashas, who wanted to be rid of us and said the weapon was sapping the strength of the army as well as bringing bad luck, but I sensed he no longer believed in victory.

That night in our tent when I tried to play something on the oud I'd managed to take along on the campaign, Hoja grabbed it from my hands and threw it aside. Did I know that they wanted my head? I knew. He said he would be a happy man if it were his head they were after instead of mine. I knew this too, but said nothing. I was about to pick up my oud again when he stopped me, asked me to tell him more about that place, my country. When I told him a couple of little fictions as I did with the sovereign, he got angry. He wanted the truth, the real facts: he asked about my mother, my fiancée, my brothers and sisters. When I began to describe the 'truth' to him he joined in, muttering hoarse words in the Italian he'd learned from me, short, incomplete sentences I couldn't make much sense of.

During the next few days, when he saw the ruined fortifications captured by our advance forces, I felt that he was desperately preoccupied by some sort of strange, foul thoughts. One morning as we were picking our way slowly through a village hit by our cannon fire, he dismounted when he saw the wounded dying in agony at the foot of a wall, and ran up to them. Watching him from a distance I thought at first that he wanted to help them, as if he would have asked them about their wounds had there been a translator with him; then I realized he was in the grip of an enthusiasm whose reason I seemed to sense; there was something else he wanted to ask them. The next day when we went with the sovereign to review the gutted fortifications and small towers on either side of the road, he was in the same excited state: he saw a wounded man whose head was still not severed from his body lying among the buildings levelled to the ground and wooden barricades riddled by cannon fire, and ran to his side. I followed him, to prevent him from doing some vile thing, afraid they would think I had put him up to it, or perhaps out of sheer base curiosity. It was as if he believed the wounded, their bodies shredded by projectiles and cannon balls, would tell him something before they drew the mask of death over their faces; Hoja was prepared to interrogate them so they might divulge it; from them he would learn that deep truth which would change everything in an instant, but I saw that he immediately identified the despair on those faces so very close to death as his own despair, and when he came close to them he couldn't speak.

That day at twilight, learning the sovereign was angry that Doppio Castle had not been captured despite all efforts, Hoja went to the sultan, again in the same state of excitement. He was apprehensive when he returned, but seemed not to know why. He had told the sultan that he wanted to send his weapon into battle, that it was for this day he'd worked on the machine so many years. The sovereign, contrary to my expectations, agreed that the moment had come, but judged it necessary to allow more time to Huseyn Pasha the Blond, whom he'd charged earlier with the assault on the castle. Why had the sovereign said this? It was one of those questions which through the years I could never be sure Hoja was asking of me or himself; for some reason I no longer felt close to him, I'd had enough of this anxiety. Hoja answered the question himself: it was because they feared he would steal a share of the victory.

Until the next afternoon, when we learned that Huseyn Pasha the Blond had still not been able to conquer the castle, Hoja squandered all his strength trying to convince himself that he was right. Since the rumours that I was accursed and a spy, I no longer went to the sovereign's tent. That night when he went to interpret the events of the day, Hoja managed to tell tales of victory and good fortune that the sultan seemed to believe. When he returned to our tent he

140

had assumed the optimistic air of a man who was confident he would break the legs of Satan in the end. As I listened to him I was struck less by his optimism than by the supreme effort he was apparently making to keep it alive.

He recounted the same old story of us and them, of the coming victory, but there was a sadness in his voice I had never heard before, accompanying these stories like a melancholy tune; it was as if he were speaking of a child-hood memory which both of us knew very well because we had shared a life together. He didn't object when I picked up my oud, nor when I clumsily jangled its strings: he was speaking of the future, of the wonderful days we would enjoy after we'd turned the river's current in the direction we wished, but we both knew he was talking about the past: visions of tranquillity appeared before my eyes, grace-ful trees in a cloistered garden behind a house, warm rooms sparkling with light, a happy family crowd gathered round a dinner table. He gave me a feeling of peace for the first time in years; I understood what he felt when he said it would be hard to leave, that he loved the people here. Then, reflecting on these people for a while, he remembered his fools and grew angry, and I felt he had good cause. It seemed his optimism was not merely an affectation; perhaps because this feeling that a new life was about to begin was something we both shared, or because I thought I'd act in the same way if I were in his place, I don't know.

The next morning when we launched our weapon, to test it, against a small enemy fortification close to the front, we both had the same uncanny premonition that it would not be much of a success. The nearly one hundred men the sovereign had provided for our support broke formation and scattered during the weapon's first assault. Some of them were crushed to bits by the weapon itself, some of them, after a few ineffective shots, were hit when the apparatus got stuck like an ass in the mud and they were left without cover. Most of them fled in fear of bad luck, and we were unable to regroup to prepare a fresh assault.

We must both have been thinking the same thing.

Later, when Hasan Pasha the Stout and his men took the fortification with scarcely a casualty inside of an hour, Hoja wanted to put that profound science to the test once again, this time with a hope I imagined I too understood quite well, but all the infidel soldiers at the fortification had fallen under the sword; there was not even a single man left drawing a last breath among the burning ruins of the barricades. And when he saw the heads piled up to one side to be taken to the sovereign, I knew at once what he was thinking; I even found his fascination justified, but by now I could not stand to see it go so far: I turned my back on him. A bit later when I looked again, overcome by curiosity, he was moving away from the stack of heads; I was never able to learn just how far he had gone.

At noon we returned to the march to hear that Doppio Castle had still not been taken. Apparently the sultan was furious, he was talking about punishing Huseyn Pasha the Blond: all of us, the whole army, would join the siege! The sovereign told Hoja that if the castle did not fall by evening our weapon would be used in the morning assault. It was then the sultan ordered that an inept commander, who had been unable all day long to take even a small fortification, should have his head cut off. The sultan had paid no attention to our weapon's failure at the fortification, news of which had by now caught up with the march, nor to the gossip about its bringing bad luck. Hoja no longer talked about sharing in the victory; although he didn't say so, I knew he was thinking about the death of the former imperial astrologer; and when I dreamed of scenes from my childhood or the animals on our estate, I knew the same things were passing through his mind; I knew that he, too, was thinking that news of a victory at the castle would be our last chance, that he didn't really believe in this chance, didn't want it. I knew there was a little church with its bell-tower ablaze in a village destroyed in rage against the castle that just could not be taken, and in that church the prayer intoned

142

by a brave priest was summoning us to a new life; that as we moved north the sun setting behind the hills of the forest awakened in him, as it did in me, a feeling of the perfection of something being silently, carefully, brought to completion.

After the sun had set and we learned not only that Huseyn Pasha the Blond had failed, but that Austrians, Hungarians, and Kazaks had joined the Poles at the siege of Doppio, we finally saw the castle itself. It was at the top of a high hill, its towers streaming with flags were caught by the faint red glow of the setting sun, and it was white; purest white and beautiful. I didn't know why I thought that one could see such a beautiful and unattainable thing only in a dream. In that dream you would run along a road twisting through a dark forest, straining to reach the bright day of that hilltop, that ivory edifice; as if there were a grand ball going on which you wanted to join in, a chance for happiness you did not want to miss, but although you expected to reach the end of the road at any moment, it would never end. When I learned that the flooding river had left a stinking swamp in the low ground between the dark woods and the foot of the slope, and that the infantry, though they were able to cross the swamp, could not get up the slope no matter how hard they tried and despite support of cannon fire, I thought of the road that had led us here. It was as if everything were as perfect as the view of that pure white castle with birds flying over its towers, as perfect as the darkening rocky cliff of the slope and the still, black forest. I knew now that many of the things I'd experienced for years as coincidence had been inevitable, that our soldiers would never be able to reach the white towers of the castle, that Hoja was thinking the same thing. I knew only too well that when we joined the siege in the morning our weapon would founder in the swamp leaving the men inside and around it to die, that as a result there would be voices demanding my head to silence the rumours of a curse, the fear, and the grumblings of soldiers, and I knew Hoja

143

realized as much. I remembered how once, years earlier, to provoke him to talk about himself, I had spoken of a childhood friend of mine with whom I'd developed the habit of thinking the same thing at the same time. I had no doubt he too was now thinking of the very same things.

Late that night he went to the sultan's tent and it seemed he would never return. For a while, since I could easily guess what he was going to say to the sovereign, who would want him to interpret for the pashas the events of the day and the future, I considered the possibility that he had been killed there on the spot and that the executioners would soon come for me. Later I imagined that he had left the tent and, without stopping to tell me, gone straight for the white towers of the castle gleaming in the dark, that having slipped past the guards, over the swamp and through the forest, he had already reached it. I was waiting for morning, thinking of my new life without much enthusiasm, when he came back. Only much later, years later, after talking at great length with those who'd been there in the sultan's tent, was I able to learn that Hoja had said just what I'd guessed he would. At the time he explained nothing to me, he was rushing about like someone about to leave on a journey. He said there was a thick fog outside. I understood.

Till the break of day I talked with him about what I'd left behind in my country, told him how he could find my house, spoke of my mother, my father, my brothers and sisters, how we were regarded in Empoli and Florence. I mentioned some tiny, special particulars by which he could know one person from another. As I spoke I recalled that I had told him all of these things before, down to the large mole on my little brother's back. At times, while entertaining the sovereign, or now while writing this book, these stories have seemed to me mere reflections of my fantasies, not the truth, but then I believed them: my sister's stutter was real, as were the many buttons on our clothes and the things I had seen from the window overlooking the garden behind our house. Towards morning I began to think I had been seduced by these stories because I believed they would continue, perhaps from where they left off, even if much later. I knew that Hoja too was thinking the same thing, that he happily believed in his own story.

We exchanged clothes without haste and without speaking. I gave him my ring and the medallion I'd managed to keep from him all these years. Inside it there was a picture of my grandmother's mother and a lock of my fiancée's hair that had gone white; I believe he liked it, he put it around his neck. Then he left the tent and was gone. I watched him slowly disappear in the silent fog. It was getting light. Exhausted, I lay down in his bed and slept peacefully.

I have now come to the end of my book. Perhaps discerning readers, deciding my story was actually finished long ago, have already tossed it aside. There was a time when I thought the same thing. I thrust these pages into a drawer years ago, intending never to read them again. In those days it was my intention to turn my mind to other stories I invented, not for the sultan but for my own pleasure, romances taking place in lands I'd never seen, in desolate wastes and frozen forests, involving a wily merchant who wandered into them like a wolf; I wanted to forget this book, this story. Though I knew it wouldn't be easy after all I'd heard and experienced, I might have succeeded if a guest hadn't come to visit me two weeks ago and persuaded me to bring my book out again. Today I know at last that of all my books this is the one I love most; I will finish it as it should be finished, as I have longed, have dreamed of doing.

From the old table where I sit finishing my book I can see a tiny sailboat ploughing the sea from Jennethisar to Istanbul, a mill turning in the distance among the olive-groves, children pushing each other as they play deep in the garden under the fig-trees, the dusty road from Istanbul to Gebze. During the winter snows few pass this way. In spring and summer I see the caravans travelling to the East, to Anatolia, even Baghdad, Damascus; I often watch the broken-down ox-carts going by at a snail's pace, and some-times I'm excited by the sight of a rider in the distance whose costume I can't identify, but when the traveller draws near I realize he is not coming to see me. In these days no one comes, and now I know no one will.

But I have no complaints, and I am not lonely: I saved a great deal of money during my years as imperial astrologer, I married, I have four children; I foresaw the troubles coming and gave up my position in time, perhaps with an insight gained from practising my profession: before the sultan's armies left for Vienna, before the fawning clowns and the imperial astrologer who succeeded me were beheaded in a frenzy of defeat, long before our sovereign who so loved animals was dethroned, I fled here to Gebze. I had this villa built and moved in with my beloved books, my children and a couple of servants. My wife, whom I married while I was still the imperial astrologer, is much younger than I, a fine housekeeper who manages the whole house and a few other minor tasks for me, and leaves me to write my books and dream, climbing towards seventy, alone all day in this room. Thus, to find an appropriate end to my story and my life, I think of Him to my heart's content.

Yet during the first years I tried never to do that. Once or twice when the sovereign had wanted to speak of Him, he realized the subject didn't attract me at all. I believe he was content to leave it that way; he was just curious; but what particularly he was curious about, and how much, I was never able to discover. At first he said I shouldn't be ashamed to have been influenced by Him, to have learned from Him. He'd known from the start that all those books, those calendars and predictions I'd presented to him over the years had been written by Him, and told Him so even when I was still struggling at home with designs for our weapon that ended up stuck in the swamp; he'd also known that He had told me this, just as I used to tell Him everything. Perhaps then both of us had not yet lost the end of the thread, but I realized the sultan had his feet more firmly on the ground than I had. In those days I thought the sovereign was cleverer than I, knew everything he was supposed to know and was toying with me so as to have me

147

more securely in the palm of his hand. And perhaps I was also influenced by the gratitude I felt to him for having rescued me from that defeat whose germ was planted in the swamp, and from the rage of the soldiers driven mad by rumours of a curse. For when they learned the infidel had escaped, some of the soldiers wanted my head. If in the first years he had asked me candidly, I believe I would have told the sultan everything. In those days the rumours that I was not who I was had not yet begun, I wanted to talk with someone about what had happened, I missed Him.

To live alone in that house we had shared for so many years unnerved me even more. My pockets full of money, my feet soon learned the way to the slave market; I went back and forth for months until I found what I sought. In the end I bought some poor devil who didn't really resemble me or Him and brought him home. That night when I told him to teach me everything he knew, to tell me about his country, his past, even to admit the sins he had committed, when I brought him to face the mirror, he was frightened of me. It was a terrible night, I pitied the poor man, I meant to set him free in the morning, but my stinginess won out and I took him to the slave market to sell him back. After that I decided to marry and let word of my intentions get out in the neighbourhood. They came gladly, thinking they would make me one of them at last, that peace would come to the street. I, too, was content to be like them, I felt optimistic, I thought the rumours had stopped, that I could live in peace inventing stories for my sovereign year after year. I chose my wife carefully; she even played the oud for me in the evenings.

When the rumours started again, I thought at first this must be another of the sultan's games, for I believed he took pleasure in observing my anxiety and asking questions that would unsettle me. In the beginning I wasn't much alarmed when he would suddenly say things to me like, 'Do we know ourselves? A man must understand who he is'; I thought he'd learned these unnerving questions from the know-it-alls interested in Greek philosophy among the sycophants he'd started to gather around him once again. When he asked me to write something on the subject, I gave him my last book about gazelles and sparrows being content because they never reflected on themselves and knew nothing of what they were. When I found that he had taken the book seriously and read it with pleasure I relaxed a bit, but the gossip began to reach my ears: it was said I treated the sultan like a fool, I did not even resemble the man whose place I had taken, He was thinner and more delicate while I had grown fat; they'd known I was lying when I said I couldn't know everything He knew; one day in time of war I, too, would bring down bad luck and then desert as He had done, I would betray secrets of state to the enemy and ease the way to defeat, etc., etc. To protect myself from these rumours that I believed the sultan had started, I withdrew from feasts and festivities, was not seen much in public, lost weight, and made careful inquiries into what had been discussed in the sovereign's tent on that last night. My wife had one child after another, my income was good, I wanted to forget the rumours, forget Him, forget the past, and continue my work in peace.

I persevered for almost seven years more; perhaps if my nerves had been stronger, or more important, if I hadn't sensed there would be another purge of the circle around the sultan, I would have gone on to the end; I would have passed through the doors the sovereign opened for me and let go of the former life I wished to forget. I was now quite shameless in answering the questions about my identity which had at first put me on guard: 'Of what importance is it who a man is?' I'd say. 'The important thing is what we have done and will do.' I believe it was through this cupboard door that the sultan got into my mind! When he asked me to tell him about Italy, about the country to which He had escaped, and I replied that I had little knowledge of it, he grew angry: he knew that He had told me everything, why was I afraid, it was enough that I should remember what He had said. So I described to the sultan in detail again His childhood and His beautiful memories, some of which I have included in this book. At first my nerves were still fairly sound, the sultan listened to me as I intended – as if listening to someone tell what he'd heard from someone else – but in later years he went further; he began listening to what I said as if it were Him speaking: he'd ask me details only He could have known, told me not to be afraid, to give the first answer that came into my head: what event was it that had precipitated His sister's stutter? Why had He not been accepted by the University of Padua? What colour clothes had His brother worn at the first fireworks display He'd seen in Venice? While I told the sovereign these details as if they had happened to me, we would be out for a day on the water, or resting by a pool teeming with frogs and water lilies, observing shameless monkeys in silver cages or strolling in one of those gardens that, because they'd walked there together, was filled with memories they shared. Then the sovereign, pleased with my stories and the play of our memories which blossomed like flowers opening in the garden, would feel closer to me and speak of Him as though recalling an old friend who had betrayed us: he said it was good He had run away, for although he found Him amusing, he'd often lost patience with His impertinence and thought of having Him killed. He revealed some things that frightened me because I couldn't quite tell which of us he was talking about, but he spoke with love, not with violence: there had been days when, unable to tolerate His self-ignorance, he feared he would have Him killed in anger – on that last night he had been on the point of calling the executioners! Later, he said I was not impertinent; I did not consider myself the most intelligent, most capable man in the world; I had not pre- sumed to interpret the terror of the plague to my own advantage; I'd not kept everyone awake at night with tales of child-kings who were impaled at the stake; and now there was no one to whom I could run home and recount and ridicule the sultan's dreams after listening to them, no one with whom I could write silly, entertaining fictions to lead him astray! As I listened I thought I saw myself, the two of us, from the outside as in a dream, and I realized that we had lost the end of the thread. But in the last months the sultan, as though to drive me mad, went on even further: I was not like Him, I had not given my mind to the sophists who distinguished between 'them' and 'us' as He had done! During the fireworks the eight-year-old sovereign had watched from the other shore before he met us, my own Devil had brought victory to that other devil in the dark sky for Him, and now had gone with Him to the land where it believed it would find peace! Later, during the walks in the garden which were always the same, the sovereign would ask thoughtfully: must one be a sultan to understand that men, in the four corners and seven climes of the world, all resembled one another? Afraid, I would say nothing; as if to break my last effort at resistance he would ask once again: was it not the best proof that men everywhere were identical with one another that they could take each other's place?

Because I hoped the sultan and I would succeed in forgetting Him one day, and because I had taken the precaution of saving more money, I might have endured this torture with patience; for I had grown used to the fear that comes with ambiguity. He opened and shut the doors of my mind mercilessly, as if riding hither and thither in pursuit of a rabbit in some forest where we'd lost our way. What's more he was now doing this in front of everyone; he was surrounded by fawning sycophants again. I was afraid because I thought there would be another purge and all of our property would be confiscated, because I sensed the troubles soon to come. It was the day he had me tell of the bridges of Venice, of the lacework on the tablecloth on which He had eaten breakfast as a child, of the view through the window overlooking the garden at the back of His house that He recalled when he was about to be beheaded for his refusal to convert to Islam – it was when the sultan ordered me to write down all of these stories in a book, as if they were my own record of what had happened to me, that I decided to escape from Istanbul as soon as possible.

I moved into a different house in Gebze so as to forget Him. At first I was afraid that palace guards would come for me, but no one sought me out, and my income was not touched; either I was forgotten, or the sovereign was having me watched secretly. I thought no more about it, I got started on my work, had this home built, landscaped the back garden as I wanted, according to my inner impulses; I passed my time reading my books, writing stories for my own pleasure and advising visitors who came to consult me because they had discovered I was a former astrologer, more for the fun of it than for their money. It was perhaps from them that I learned most about my country where I have lived from childhood: before I agreed to tell the fortunes of cripples, or men bewildered at the loss of a son or brother, the chronically ill, the fathers of girls left unmarried, men who never grew to their full height, jealous husbands, the blind, sailors, and hopeless lovers with wild eyes, I'd make them tell me their life stories at length, and at night I would write down what I'd heard in notebooks so as to use them later in my stories, just as I have done with this book.

It was in those years, too, that I met the old man who brought a profound melancholy with him into my room. He must have been ten, fifteen years older than I. As soon as I saw the sadness in the face of this man called Evliya*, I decided that loneliness was his trouble, but he didn't say that: it seems he'd devoted his whole life to wandering and the ten-volume book of travels he was about to finish. Before he died he meant to make the journey to the place closest to God, to Mecca and Medina, and write about them as well, but there was something missing in his book that

* Evliya Chelebi (c. 1611–82) is the author of the renowned *Book of Travels (Seyahatname)* – Trans.

disturbed him, he wanted to tell his readers about the fountains and bridges of Italy whose beauty he'd heard so much about, and he wondered whether I, whom he'd come to see because of my fame in Istanbul, might be able to tell him about them? When I said I'd never seen Italy, he declared that he knew that as well as anyone else, but had heard I'd once had a slave who came from there, who had described everything to me; if I would in turn tell Evliya, he would repay me with amusing anecdotes: wasn't inventing and listening to diverting stories the pleasantest part of life? As he shyly took a map from his case, the worst map of Italy I'd ever seen, I decided to tell him what he wanted.

With his childish, pudgy hand, he started pointing out cities on the map and after pronouncing each name syllable by syllable, wrote down carefully the descriptions I gave him. For every city he wanted a curious tale as well. Passing thirteen nights in thirteen cities in this way, we traversed from north to south the whole of this land I was seeing for the first time in my life, then returned to Istanbul by the boat from Sicily. Thus we spent the entire morning. He was so pleased with what I had told him that he decided to give me pleasure too, and told me about the tightrope-walkers disappearing into the skies of Acre, the woman of Konya who gave birth to an elephant, the blue-winged bulls by the shores of the Nile, pink cats, the clock-tower of Vienna, the false front teeth he'd had made there and which he now displayed in a grin, the talking cave on the beach of the Sea of Azov, the red ants of America. For some reason these stories prompted a strange melancholy, I felt like crying. The red glow of the setting sun flooded my room. When Evliya asked if I, too, had amazing tales like these, I thought I'd really surprise him and invited him and his servants to stay the night: I had a story that would delight him, about two men who had exchanged lives.

The night after everyone else had retired to their rooms, after the silence we both waited for had fallen over the house, we returned to the room once more. It was then I

153

first imagined this tale you are about to finish! The story I told seemed not to have been made-up but actually lived, it was as if someone else were softly whispering all these words to me, the sentences slowly following one another in sequence: 'We were sailing from Venice to Naples when the Turkish fleet appeared...'

Long after midnight, when my story was finished, there was a prolonged silence. I sensed that we were both thinking of Him, but in Evliya's mind there was a Him completely different from the one in mine. I have no doubt he was actually thinking of his own life! And I, I was thinking of my own life, of Him, of how I loved the story I'd created; and I felt pride in everything I had lived and dreamed of: the room we were sitting in overflowed with the sad memories of all that both of us had once wanted to be and what we had become; it was then I understood clearly for the first time that I would never again be able to forget Him, that this would make me unhappy for the rest of my days; I knew then that I would never be able to live alone: it was as if in the dead of night, along with my story, the shadow of an alluring phantom had fallen across the room, arousing our curiosity while it put us both on guard. Near dawn, my guest delighted me by saying he'd loved my story, but added that he had to disagree with certain details. Perhaps to escape the unnerving memory of my twin and to return again as quickly as possible to my new life, I gave him all my attention.

He agreed that we must seek the strange and surprising, as in my story; yes, perhaps this was the one thing we could do to combat the exhausting tedium of this world; because he had known this ever since those monotonous years of childhood and school, he had never in his life ever considered withdrawing within four walls; that's why he had spent his whole life travelling, searching for stories down roads that never came to an end. But we should search for the strange and surprising in the world, not within ourselves! To search within, to think so long and hard about our own selves, would only make us unhappy. This is what had happened to the characters in my story: for this reason heroes could never tolerate being themselves, for this reason they always wanted to be someone else. Let us suppose that what happened in my story were true. Did I believe that those two men who had taken each other's places could be happy in their new lives? I was silent. Later, for some reason or other, he reminded me of one detail in my story: we must not allow ourselves to be led astray by the hopes of a one-armed Spanish slave! If we did, little by little, by writing those kinds of tales, by searching for the strange within ourselves, we, too, would become someone else, and God forbid, our readers would too. He did not even want to think about how terrible the world would be if men spoke always of themselves, of their own peculiarities, if their books and their stories were always about this.

But I wanted to! So when this little old man I'd come to love in just one day gathered together his attendants at dawn for the journey to Mecca, and took to the road, I sat down at once and wrote out my story. For the sake of my readers in that terrible world to come, I did all I could to make both myself and Him, whom I could not separate from myself, come alive in the story. But recently, while looking again at what I'd tossed aside sixteen years before, I thought I had not been very successful. So I apologize to those readers who don't like it when a man speaks of himself – especially when he's caught up in such confusing emotions – and add these pages to my book:

I loved Him, I loved Him the way I loved that helpless, wretched ghost of my own self I saw in my dreams, as if choking on the shame, rage, sinfulness, and melancholy of that ghost, as if overcome with shame at the sight of a wild animal dying in pain, or enraged by the selfishness of a spoilt son of my own. And perhaps most of all I loved Him with the stupid revulsion and stupid joy of knowing myself; my love for Him resembled the way I had become used to the futile insect-like movements of my hands and arms, the way I understood the thoughts which every day echoed against the walls of my mind and died away, the way I recognized the unique smell of sweat from my wretched body, my thinning hair, ugly mouth, the pink hand holding my pen: it was for this reason they had not been able to deceive me. After I had written my book and, so I'd forget Him, tossed it aside, I was never taken in by any of the rumours that were circulating, the games of those who had heard of our fame and wanted to take advantage of it – not at all! Some pasha in Cairo had taken Him under his wing and now He was making designs for a new weapon! He had been inside the city walls of Vienna during the unsuccessful siege, advising the enemy how to rout us completely! He'd been seen in Edirne disguised as a beggar, and during a quarrel among merchants that He himself had stirred up, He'd knifed a quilter and disappeared! He was the imam of a neighbourhood mosque in a distant Anatolian village, He'd set up a clock-room – those who told this story swore it was true; and He'd begun collecting money for a clock-tower! He'd become rich writing books in Spain, where he'd gone following the plague! They even said it was He who had conspired to have our poor sovereign dethroned! He was living in Slav villages, where he was treated with great respect as a legendary epileptic priest, writing books full of despair based on the true confessions He'd at last been able to hear! He was wandering around Anatolia, saying He'd overthrow those fools of sultans, leading a gang he'd bewitched with his predictions and poetry, and was calling for me to join Him! During those sixteen years when I wrote stories so as to forget Him, so as to distract myself with those terrifying people and their terrifying worlds of the future, to experience the full delights of my fantasies, I heard many more variations of these rumours, but I didn't believe any of them. I don't know, I wonder whether it happens to others: sometimes, when we felt imprisoned by those four walls at the far reaches of the Golden Horn, sometimes, waiting for an invitation which never seemed to come from a mansion or from the palace, relishing our hatred for each other, or grinning at one another while we wrote yet another treatise for our sovereign, in the little things of daily life, at the same moment, both of us would fasten upon one small detail: a wet dog we'd seen together in the rain that morning, the hidden geometry in the colours and shapes of a line of laundry hung between two trees, a slip of the tongue that suddenly brought out life's symmetry! These are the moments I miss most! And for this reason I have returned to the book of my shadow, imagining that some curious person will read it years, perhaps hundreds of years after His death, and picture his own life rather than ours; this book that I really wouldn't much care if no one ever read, and where I have hidden His name, buried, if not very deeply, inside it: so that I might once more dream of the nights of the plague, of my childhood in Edirne, of the delightful hours I'd spent in the sultan's gardens, of the first time I saw Him unbearded at the pasha's door, of the chill down my spine. To lay hands again upon the life and the dreams we lost, everyone understands the need to dream of these things again: I believed in my story!

I will conclude my book by telling of the day I decided to finish it: two weeks ago, while I sat again at our table, trying to dream up a different story, I saw a rider approaching from the Istanbul road. No one had brought me news of Him lately, perhaps because I was so brusque with my visitors that I hardly imagined they would come any more, but as soon as I caught sight of that traveller wearing a cape and carrying a parasol in his hand, I knew he was coming to see me. I heard his voice before he entered my room, he was speaking Turkish with His errors, though with not so many as He did, but as soon as he entered my room he switched to Italian. When he saw my face go sour and that I gave no answer, he said in his bad Turkish he'd thought I would at least know a little Italian. Later he explained he'd learned my name and who I was from Him. After returning to His country He had written a stack of books describing

157

His unbelievable adventures among the Turks, about their last sovereign who so loved animals and his dreams, about the plague and the Turkish people, our customs at court and at war. With curiosity about the exotic Orient just beginning to spread among aristocrats and especially well-bred ladies, His writings were well-received, His books much read, He gave lectures in the universities, and grew rich. Moreover, His former fiancée, swept up in the romanticism of His writings, married him without giving a thought to her age or her husband's recent death. They bought back the old family home which had been broken up and sold, and settled down there, returning the house and its garden to their former state. My guest knew all this because, having admired His books, he'd visited Him at home. He had been very polite, gave the visitor His whole day and answered his questions, told once again the adventures He'd written about in His books. It was then He'd spoken of me at length: He was writing a book about me with the title 'A Turk of My Acquaintance'; He was about to present my whole life to His Italian readers, from my childhood in Edirne to the day He left, supported by His cleverly written personal interpretations of the peculiarities of the Turks. 'You told Him such a great deal about yourself!' my guest said. Later, to intrigue me even more, he recalled details from what little he'd read of the book: I had been ashamed after mercilessly beating up one of my childhood friends from the neighbourhood and wept with regret, I was intelligent, I had in six months understood all the astronomy He taught me, I loved my sister very much, I was fond of my religion, I performed my prayers regularly, I adored cherry preserves, I had a particular interest in quilting, my stepfather's profession, like all Turks I loved people, etc., etc. After he had shown so much interest in me, I knew I couldn't behave inhospitably to this fool and a traveller like him was sure to be interested, so I showed him my house, room by room. Later he became fascinated by the games my sons were playing with their friends in the garden; he wrote down in a notebook the rules of tipcat and blindman's bluff, which he made them explain to him, and leapfrog, though he didn't much like that game. It was then he said that He was an admirer of the Turks. While I showed him around our garden, for lack of anything else to do, and then the miserable town of Gebze and the house where I'd stayed with Him years before, he said it again. While examining our pantry, among the jars of preserves and pickles, the jugs of olive oil and vinegar, which rather interested him, he saw my portrait in oil that I'd commissioned from a Venetian painter and further confided, as if he were betraying a secret, that actually He was not a true friend of the Turks, that He'd written unflattering things about them: He'd written that we were now in decline, described our minds as if they were dirty cupboards filled with old junk. He'd said we could not be reformed, that if we were to survive our only alternative was to submit immediately, and after this we would not be able to do anything for centuries but imitate those to whom we had surrendered. 'But He wanted to save us,' I put in, wishing he would stop, and he responded at once saying yes, for our sake He had even built a weapon, but we had not understood Him; on a foggy morning the machine had been left stuck in a disgusting swamp like the awesome corpse of a pirate ship marooned in a storm. Then he added: yes, He had indeed wanted, very much, to save us. This did not mean there was no evil in Him. All genius was like that! While carefully examining my portrait which he'd picked up, he was mumbling a few more things about genius: if He had not fallen into slavery at our hands but instead lived a life in His own country, He might even have been the Leonardo of the seventeenth century. Later he returned to his favourite subject of evil, passing on one or two nasty pieces of gossip about Him and money which I had heard but since forgotten. 'The strange thing,' he said later, 'is that you have not been affected by Him at all!' He said he'd come to know and love me; he expressed his astonishment:

159

how two people who'd lived together so many years could resemble each other so little, how they could be so unlike one another, he could not understand. He didn't ask for my portrait, as I'd feared he would; after putting it back he asked if he could see the quilts. 'What quilts?' I said, bewildered. He was surprised: didn't I pass my free time by stitching quilts? It was then I decided to show him the book I had not touched in sixteen years.

At this he became agitated, said he could read Turkish, that of course he was very interested in any book about Him. We went up to my work-room overlooking the garden. He sat at our table, and I found my book where I had, as if yesterday, thrust it away sixteen years before; I laid it open before him. He was able to read Turkish, if slowly. He buried himself in the book with that desire to be swept away without leaving one's own sane and secure world which I'd seen in all travellers, and despised. I left him alone, I went out into the garden and sat down on the divan covered with straw matting where I could see him through the open window. At first he was cheerful and called out to me from the window, 'How obvious it is you have never set foot in Italy!' But he soon forgot me; I sat in the garden for three hours, glancing up at him occasionally out of the corner of my eye as I waited for him to finish the book. By then he had understood, though there was confusion on his face; once or twice he called out the name of the white castle behind the swamp that had swallowed up our weapon; he even tried in vain to speak Italian with me. Then he turned and gazed blankly out of the window, resting and trying to digest what he'd read. I watched with delight as he looked first at some infinite point in the emptiness, as people do in such situations, at some non-existent focal point, but then, then, as I had expected, his vision focused: now he was looking at the scene through the frame of the window. My intelligent readers have surely understood: he was not so stupid as I supposed. As I had thought he would, he began to turn the pages of my book greedily, searching, and I waited with excitement till at last he found the page he was looking for and read it. Then he looked again at the view from that window overlooking the garden behind my house. I knew exactly what he saw. Peaches and cherries lay on a tray inlaid with mother-of-pearl upon a table, behind the table was a divan upholstered with straw matting, strewn with feather cushions the same colour as the green window frame. I was sitting there, nearly seventy now. Further back, he saw a sparrow perched on the edge of a well among the olive and cherry trees. A swing tied with long ropes to a high branch of a walnut-tree swayed slightly in a barely perceptible breeze.

1984–85

About the Translator

Victoria Holbrook lived in Istanbul for five years and is currently Assistant Professor of Turkish Literature at Ohio State University.

ALSO BY ORHAN PAMUK

THE NEW LIFE

"I read a book one day, and my whole life was changed."
Thus begins this brilliant novel in which the narrator,
Osman, finds a book that allows him to glimpse both
international conspiracy and the possibility of eternal love.
His obsessive experience with the book mysteriously links
him with the ethereally beautiful Janan and together they
embark upon a search for her missing lover, Mehmet, who is
also obsessed with the book. *The New Life* plays out in a
mysterious dreamlike landscape that is part Turkish, part
American and wholly original.

"Timeless and moving. . . . With [his] fusion of literary
elegance and incisive political commentary, Pamuk drew
comparisons to Salman Rushdie and Don DeLillo. Here, he
confirms that talent, brilliantly chronicling his hapless hero's
search for love, revenge and life beyond the postmodern
novel."   —*Publishers Weekly*

Fiction/Literature/0-375-70171-0

VINTAGE INTERNATIONAL
Available at your local bookstore, or call toll-free to order:
1-800-793-2665 (credit cards only).